Destruction
at
Noonday

Books by Bill Robinson

The Science of Sailing
New Boat
A Berth to Bermuda
Where the Trade Winds Blow
Expert Sailing
Over the Horizon
The World of Yachting
The Best from Yachting *(Editor)*
Better Sailing for Boys and Girls
The America's Cup Races *(co-author)*
Legendary Yachts
The Sailing Life
The Right Boat for You
Great American Yacht Designers
America's Sailing Book
A Sailor's Tales
Cruising: The Boats and the Places
South to the Caribbean
Where to Cruise
Islands
Caribbean Cruising Handbook
Eighty Years of Yachting
Cruising the Easy Way
Best Sailing Spots Worldwide

Destruction at Noonday

BILL ROBINSON

SHERIDAN HOUSE

Copyright © 1992 by Bill Robinson

Published by Sheridan House Inc.
145 Palisade Street
Dobbs Ferry, NY 10522

Library of Congress Cataloging-in-Publication Data

Robinson, Bill, 1918-
     Destruction at noonday / Bill Robinson.
        p.   cm.
     ISBN 0-924486-21-X : $22.95
     I. Title.
PS3568.0284D47 1992
813'.54—dc20   92-7250
                                                       CIP

Design by Jeremiah B. Lighter
Manufactured in the United States of America
ISBN 0-924486-21-X

The destruction that wasteth at noonday
Psalms 91:1–6

AUTHOR'S NOTE:
The nautical events here approximate what actually went on in the Yokohama earthquake of 1923, but the characters and their involvements are entirely fictional.

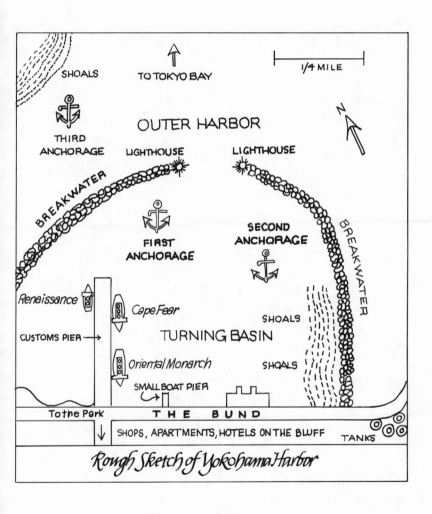

Rough Sketch of Yokohama Harbor

To my cousin Bob

PART

I

F ROM THE WINDOW, looking over the rooftops below him and across the Bund and the shoreline to the long ribbon of the Customs pier jutting northward into the harbor, his glance went automatically to the great bulk of the *Oriental Monarch* dominating the other ships berthed there. The 615 feet of her graceful white hull, the high superstructure, and three buff funnels towered over a freighter astern of her and a smaller passenger liner on the other side of the pier. As always, there was that quick burst of pride at the sight of his ship, a handsome vessel and the largest liner in the Pacific. At the same time, the corner of his eye caught the white of his uniform jacket hanging on the outside of the closet—a reminder that it was time to be getting back on board.

The thought of putting on clothes was a reluctant one as a puff of humid breeze through the window touched his naked flesh. The air was heavy with a smoky reminder of industry and waterfront pungency, mixed with cooking smells and a suggestion of spices. He shifted his gaze from the ships to the clouds, the horizon of Tokyo Bay beyond the Yokohama breakwaters, and the surface of the harbor. His seaman's eye disliked what it saw, even though it was now obvious that the typhoon that had been on the north coast and headed out over the Sea of Japan yesterday had not changed from that predicted course. If it had,

Chin Ching would have come for him immediately. He always told his steward where he would be when he went ashore.

There was a dirty, hazy look to the sky, and the sun had not yet broken through a band of black on the horizon, while low, gray clouds scudded out of the southeast. The harbor water had a hard, metallic sheen, and darker blotches skittered across it where wind gusts hit the surface. Though this was just the fringe of the typhoon, the weather was unsettled, with an uneasiness in the air, and it would be a source of anxiety until the ship sailed at noon.

"Why have you left me?" Mikaela's voice came across the room from the bed behind him, sleep blurring the lilt of her Swedish accent.

"Duty, duty, duty, my dear—" He gave a short laugh, turning to face her, and the blocky bulk of his body silhouetted against the light.

Mikaela yawned and stretched. "Come back to me, please. For a minute; I haven't kissed you this morning."

He gave a deep chuckle as he turned and sank to the edge of the bed, and she rose from the tangle of silken sheets and came into his arms, her flesh warm and her hair soft against his cheek and shoulders. They kissed tenderly, then harder.

Leaning away, she murmured "God damn duty. God damn it," then kissed him again. "Now you will go back to your great ship and be God again in your beautiful white uniform and your gold stripes and your captain's hat. It is so hard to remember how grand a captain you are when you are with me like this, my love, my beautiful man of muscle. Do you know you are like a little boy when you are making love?"

"Not too little, I hope," he growled, and she punched him lightly on the chest. "But I am, I am a boy again; you make me feel like one, but nothing like this ever happened when I was a boy."

"I wish I'd known you then."

"If I'd only known that there could be someone like you when I was young. What a difference—" His voice muffled as he buried his head into the warm softness of her breast and shoulder and she cradled it.

After a moment, she spoke into the clipped gray of his hair. "Now we know, don't we? But how could I ever have guessed the first time I saw Captain Samuel Applebye so stern and commanding on the bridge of his ship that we would ever be like this. And, oh, it is such a short time, and you will be gone for so long."

"That's what happens when you tangle with a sailor."

"What day will it be?"

"September 25th, typhoons willing, *Oriental Monarch* will steam into Yokohama and I will steam into your arms again, and then it's only a week to Hong Kong and back, so we'll be together three times in a month—almost."

"I will mark the day on my calendar," she said. "Yesterday I had a great red circle around August 31st, 1923. Now I will live for the next red circle."

"Mikaela, my darling," he said, lifting his head and looking into her eyes, "all my life I have lived for ships and the sea. The days ashore have been marking time—interruptions. For the first time, I'm looking at it the other way. I don't want to leave you."

"You have a wife, a house in Canada."

"I have had more love with you in one day than in twenty years with her. She doesn't know what love is—and I didn't either. Let's say we have been a convenience to each other. I've had less and less to do with women in recent years until you—you—woke me up."

"Sailors are supposed to do wild things when they are in port."

✳ 5 ✳

"Sailors, maybe, and maybe sometimes. But not often masters of passenger liners. And at fifty-two I shouldn't be thinking of such things."

"Fifty-two is a lovely age. You look so handsome and distinguished but your body is young and hard." She kissed him. "And you are a wonderful lover."

"You have made me one," he murmured. "How you've taught me." They clung to each other. Breaking away, he shook his head. "But now I must go."

She moaned, held him tight for a moment and then fell back, her hair a golden skein across the pillow. "Yes. You must. You must. And I cannot be late to the consulate, either. We have some people sailing on your ship, and I must have their passports and visas ready."

Her apartment was in a European-style building on the Bund, the harborfront boulevard, and the bathtub had a showerhead on a spindly pipe, closed in by a curtain on a ring. His shoulders bulged the curtain as he stood under the water, rinsing off the stickiness and bringing back the memories of the night. Small shivers shook him and there was an inward chuckle of self-congratulation deep in his throat at the thought of what had happened, the wonder at the unbelievable twist in his ordered life.

He put on the uniform, now mussed and wrinkled, while Mikaela splashed in the tub. She had dried and was fragrant with powder when he was ready to leave, and a last tender kiss ended in a desperate hug.

"Goodbye, my captain. Come back safely. And *tak* for love."

"*Tak* for you." He took the curve of her chin between his fingers, gazed straight and deep into her eyes and gave a small squeeze. "Thank God for you."

Two flights of stairs put him onto a side street off the Bund in the oppressive humidity and mix of seaport smells. Normally he would have enjoyed the half-mile walk to the ship, but the sweat was already rolling down the small of his back, and he hailed a rickshaw.

The breeze through the porthole was warm and humid with a pungent mixture of harbor water, smoke and soot, and the hidden spices of Yokohama, as Chin Ching, in white steward's jacket and black pantaloons, padded noiselessly around the sitting room of the captain's quarters. The sun, breaking through a band of dirty haze in the east, plated the molten gray of the harbor, and small puffs of clouds scudded out of the southeast from the hills beyond the waterfront, their dark shadows chasing each other across the surface. The typhoon that had worried the captain last evening would not hit them now, Chin Ching knew, and there had been no need for him to go for the captain.

He could see the building where the Swedish woman had her apartment outlined on "the Bluff," the foreign quarter above the Bund, and he wondered whether the captain was awake and on his way back. A fresh white uniform and clean underwear were on the bunk where he had laid them out, with whitened shoes underneath.

Now he began to dust the already spotless quarters, gently touching each vase and figurine, all carefully secure in their racks for going to sea, and the tapestries, prints and photographs above the desk. He was as proud of the collection of Oriental art objects as the captain was, and he had developed an intense personal interest in tending it. He had even found a few of the items himself in small shops he knew in Hong Kong, and he took great pleasure in how happy this had made the captain.

As he dusted the desk and papers which Captain Applebye always kept in neat, orderly piles, he was surprised to see that a letter from Mrs. Applebye, which had come in from Canada on a westbound ship and had been delivered aboard

the day before, was still unopened, lying where Chin Ching
had placed it. He knew the captain had seen it, but obviously he had ignored it while he was getting ready to go ashore
last night. Chin Ching frowned slightly and raised his eyes
to the photograph of Mrs. Applebye, with her handsome
face, severe line of mouth, and proud, direct gaze. Although
she had always treated him with cool, offhand formality and
condescension whenever she came aboard the ship in
Vancouver, he had a sense that his loyalty to the captain
should also include the family, and the unopened letter
disturbed him.

There was a rap on the door to the wing of the bridge,
and he moved to it and opened it quietly. Staff Captain
Robertshaw, in crisp whites, had his hand raised to knock
again, and he held it in midair while his pale gray eyes
stared at the impassive face of the Chinaman.

"Is the captain aboard yet?"

"No sir, Mister Lobbyshaw."

Robertshaw frowned in annoyance at the Chinese cor-
ruption of his name.

"Did he tell you when he would be back?" His voice
was loud, and he spaced his words distinctly as though he
were talking to a deaf person.

"No sir, Mister Lobbyshaw."

"But do you know where he is?"

"Yes sir, Mister Lobbyshaw."

"Dammit, man, I know my own name. Well if he is not
here soon, I shall have to send you for him. We sail in three
hours, and there are things to be done."

"Yes sir, Mister Lobbyshaw. He come soon, I am sure.
Maybe I help you?"

"No no. Nothing for you to do. But I want to know the
moment he comes aboard." His cold gaze held on Chin
Ching in an attempt to stare him down.

"Yes sir, Mister Lobbyshaw."

Robertshaw continued his stare for a few seconds, frowned, and turned quickly away. Chin Ching watched him without moving until the white top of his officer's cap disappeared down the bridge ladder, then closed the door softly and went back to his dusting. His face was still bland and expressionless, but there was a hint of glitter in the black eyes as he moved about the cabin.

The rickshaw came down out of the side street and turned left onto the Bund. Sam Applebye's glance went immediately to the *Oriental Monarch* when her big white hull and towering buff stacks came into view, dominating the ships around her as she lay starboard side to her berth, facing the shore, almost at the end of the 1,800-yard-long Customs pier. Again, the sight of his ship brought that surge of pride. Ever since his first command—the tough, scruffy little cargo ship *Mirs Bay*—looking at his ship had always given him a special private thrill he would never admit to in so many words. It was a hangover of boyish excitement from his first days at sea, and the *Monarch*, especially, brought out the secret thrill. She was the largest liner in the Pacific, and the largest ever to transit the Panama Canal.

With the ship in view, he tried to shift his thoughts to the sailing hour and the routines in between, but Mikaela, the memory of her, and of her presence, was still with him. He could sense her fragrance, the softness of her hair, and it came to him sharply that he had to keep her in his life somehow. Single nights twice a month when the ship stopped in Yokohama seemed like nothing at all, and her tour of duty at the Swedish consulate would not last more than a year or two. How could he expect an attractive women of thirty-three to build her life around his brief visits? She had said that there was no one else, that she was just beginning to get over the shock of being widowed when she came

aboard the ship as a passenger on her way out to Japan, and
that he was the first man since her husband had died. But
what right did he have to make any demands? What had he
to offer?

If he divorced Alicia to marry her, that would finish
him with the Canada & Orient Steamship Company. Alicia's
brother Julian was a director, a supporter now who would
turn into an implacable enemy, just when his ordered life
seemed to be reaching a climax. The bigger, faster *Pacific
Monarch*, new flagship of the C & O would join the fleet in
a few months, and he would normally be in line to command
her as the senior C & O captain. There was only the
incident of the *Oriental Monarch* ticking her propeller on a
rock at the entrance to Vancouver when the harbor pilot
was bringing her in two voyages past. Even though the pilot
was in charge, it was still the captain's ship and the incident
would be a minor note on his otherwise flawless record.
That was probably why Robertshaw had been assigned as
staff captain—a company spy to keep an eye on him. Fishy-
eyed bastard, coldly correct at every turn, so efficient it
hurt.

Sam shook his head and passed a hand over his eyes.
Life was not simple any more, the way it had been for so
many years, after the one rash move that had brought him
out to the Pacific. As a young third mate on the little coastal
steamer owned by his grandfather's company, his future had
been secure, but the North Sea run out of Hull in Yorkshire
was dull; the North Sea was cold, rough and nasty, the ports
were drab, and there was no excitement in coming ashore
on his days off to the staid Victorian atmosphere of his
parents' home. His father had dressed him down one day,
treating him like a child, and he had spent a long evening
drinking ale with his chum, Jack Pearson. Jack had a dull
job in the Post Office and was fuming after a similar
blow-up with his own father.

"Treats me like a bloody baby," Jack had muttered. "I've had enough. I'm off for Canada," he told Sam, tossing off his half-pint in one angry swig. "That I am. I'm not one for withering away in the old P.O. and having my Pa treat me like I'm still in grammar school. There's gold to be had in Canada and I'm going after it. How's to come with me?"

Sam had felt a quick surge of excitement, a flash of reckless abandon. "By God, I will, Jack. There'll be hell to pay at home, but I'm with you."

Hell to pay there was as he had been expected to work his way up in the family company—but his mind was made up, and, after a row of a scene he and Jack were off, working their way across the Atlantic and Canada.

Reality set in rapidly in the British Columbia gold fields. There were more miners than good claims, and their small cash reserve melted away while they slaved without success. Then Jack came down with a high fever, and, while Sam watched helplessly, unable to find a doctor, worsened and died in three days. It was a scared, broke and depressed young sailor, haunted by the last lost look in Jack's eyes, who made his way down to Vancouver, hoping to get some sort of seafaring berth. By a stroke of good timing his mate's ticket got him a berth as fourth officer on the C & O freighter *Northland*, replacing a man who had just had an appendicitis attack, and he made up his mind to stick to his profession. As he worked his way up the company ladder, marriage to Alicia seemed like a smart convenience for both of them, as she was already past thirty, with an austere manner that had frightened off all suitors. She had her house, her garden, and her good works in charity—and Sam had an inside track with the company. Until now it had been a satisfactory arrangement.

The rickshaw turned onto the road leading along the

pier. The *Monarch*'s high bow loomed over the supply trucks and the taxis and private autos bringing passengers and their friends out to the ship. It was a busy, crowded scene as the rickshaw boy threaded his way to the gangway.

In a reflex action, Dr. Richard Holden straightened his tie and smoothed his hair back before knocking on the door of the Hong Kong Suite. The door was opened by a heavy-set woman with black hair pulled straight back, heavy eyebrows, and a questioning look on her face.

"I'm—I'm the doctor. Doctor Holden."

She gazed at him without expression for a moment, then stepped back.

"Yes. Miss Clare is expecting you."

The Hong Kong Suite, one of four on the ship, was done in heavy oriental style, dark and ornate, and the atmosphere was closed in and perfumed. He had seen Madelaine Clare in some of her movies, a lively, bright-eyed girl with a flashing smile, and he was not prepared for the pale, soft woman sitting quietly on a settee.

"Here's the doctor, Madelaine," the woman announced and left the room.

"Oh. Yes." She looked up with a hint of a smile. "Thank you for coming."

"You asked to see me. Do you have a problem?" He found it difficult to connect this quiet, almost tremulous woman with the vivid image she created on the screen. Though pale, she was lovely looking, with auburn hair and large, beautiful eyes, but he could see that she was beyond the youthful image her movie roles had given.

"Well, it's not a crisis," her voice was soft and low, "but I do need something." She smiled directly at him, her eyes fully on him, and they had a moist, luminous look. She seemed to be appealing to him as a man, rather than as a doctor. "I wonder if you could provide me with some paregoric?"

"Paregoric?" He couldn't hide his surprise.

"Yes. I usually travel with some—in case my stomach is upset—and my bottle fell in the sink and broke. It's a terrible nuisance, but I thought you might have some."

"Well, yes, I think I do. I don't get many calls for it, but I must have some. I'll have to look. Do you have any special symptoms now?"

"Well, I have been a bit upset, yes. Nothing terrible, but I would feel better with some."

"I'll have to go to my office. I'll be right back and let you know."

"If you don't have any, could you get some on shore before we sail?"

"Well, possibly. I'll check my office."

"You're a dear man, and thank you." She flashed him her onscreen smile and her face took on new life.

"I'll be back." He turned and left the room and she sat back quietly with a sigh. The heavy woman came in from one of the two cabins off the sitting room.

"How about it?" she asked.

"He's going to see. My, I thought a ship's doctor would be old, a retired type. He's a young looking man. Quite handsome, but he looks tired."

Holden closed the door behind him and started down the passageway. Paregoric! My God, he thought. I've heard of little old ladies having to have it prescribed for them, but I've never run into it before. Opium in it; that's what does it. She must be in tough shape. The image of her doe-eyed, vulnerable look and the flash of her smile were vividly with him as he walked down the passageway. And who was he, he thought wryly, to criticize someone with a dependency.

*   *   *

Robertshaw stood at the chart table in the bridge impatiently tapping a pair of dividers against the chart and watching the door to the wing. When Fourth Mate Perkins came quickly through it, stumbling for a moment on the sill, Robertshaw glanced at his watch.

"It's about time, Mr. Perkins."

Perkins came to a stop next to him and put the watch bill down on the table. Rivulets of sweat ran down his cheeks from his temples.

"Your uniform is wrinkled and damp, Mr. Perkins—are you going to a fire?" Robertshaw asked.

Perkins frowned and gave a nervous little laugh. "Sorry, sir. It is quite warm."

Robertshaw studied the watch bill that assigned bridge duty, obviously looking for a mistake, then tossed it back onto the table. "Next time I would like it here at oh-eight-hundred of sailing day. There's no excuse to be this late."

"Yes sir."

"You know you're on trial, and there can be no more mistakes."

"Yes sir."

"Go about your duties now."

"Yes sir." Perkins left as quickly as possible, feeling the staff captain's hard stare on his back as he ducked through the door. Would the man ever give him a moment's peace? Captain Applebye was much more understanding and helpful, strict as he was, and severe as he had been over the lifeboat incident. Perkins shuddered inwardly at the memory of his turning back in panic to the safety of the ship berthed in Hong Kong on the previous voyage when the fringes of a typhoon were lashing the harbor. A small coastal schooner had been in serious trouble, dragging anchor and taking on water, drifting towards the sea wall, and Perkins had been sent in charge of the motor lifeboat to try to help the vessel. With the lifeboat yawing wildly and taking on water, instead of pressing on to the schooner he had turned back, and the little ship had been dashed against the wall, breaking up quickly, with her crew drowned in the crashing waves.

It had been his first big moment of responsibility, and he still could not understand the sudden panic that had gripped him, a panic that had wiped out everything but the thought of safety back on the *Oriental Monarch*. Captain Applebye had condemned him stonily with a quick dressing down, but had not mentioned the incident since and was always helpful in making sure Perkins was doing things the right way. It was Robertshaw who never let him forget it, and was always finding fault with everything he did.

While he made his way along the promenade deck toward the gangway, his station during boarding hours, Perkins noticed the deck steward beginning to put his chairs out. A few passengers who had boarded in Hong Kong lined the rail watching the scene on the pier below, where Yokohama passengers were beginning to queue up for boarding. There was the usual jumble of taxis and rickshaws arriving, crewmembers bringing trunks and suitcases to the baggage chute, stewards lined up by the gangway to lead passengers to their cabins, and a general air of excitement and expectancy that always mounted as sailing hour approached. All the crewmembers were Chinese. Captain Applebye had made sure that they were the only kind of crew he wanted, the most conscientious and loyal imaginable, and Perkins had found this to be so as long as they knew their orders and duties.

When he neared the gangway, Perkins noticed a disturbance at the land end of it, where a large, flamboyantly dressed man was making quite a scene out of kissing a woman goodbye, at the same time engaging in some sort of argument with the porters handling his luggage.

As the rickshaw threaded through the tangle of activity on the pier, Sam noticed the confusion at the land end of the gangway. He stopped the rickshaw boy, settled with him quickly, and walked ahead to where someone was blocking people trying to go up the gangplank. A beefy man in a white suit, white shoes, Panama hat, and bright Ascot tie had one arm around a woman, holding her close against him, and was gesticulating with a cane in his other hand at a pair of crewmembers standing by his luggage.

"No! No!" he bellowed. "That case is to come aboard with me. The others can go to the baggage room. That one, you idiot!" He brandished his cane toward one bag as the porter was picking up another one. "Does anyone here understand English?" He turned and planted a wet, nuzzly kiss on the woman's neck, murmuring something to her before breaking off and shouting again at the porters, "Do you understand, blockheads?"

His face was florid and heavy, with a large chin, thick, wet lips, eyes that glittered black, and a fringe of black curly hair on his neck beneath the Panama.

Applebye summoned the purser who was standing by the gangway entrance, his mouth open in an ineffectual attempt to settle the situation.

"Who is that man?" Sam asked the purser.

"His name is Sergei Davidoff, sir."

"Ah, yes. I had word he was coming. A financier of some sort, I believe. Well, we have to break up his scene. Is the woman a passenger?"

"No sir. He is boarding by himself, but she came in his limousine with him."

"See to him," Sam ordered the purser.

The purser closed with Davidoff, who was again enveloping the woman in a smothering embrace and making loud smacking noises as he kissed her. "Excuse me, Mr. Davidoff; could we please clear the gangway so that other—"

"When I'm ready," Davidoff said coldly, without turning his head.

Sam stepped forward, close to the couple, and spoke firmly. "How do you do, Mr. Davidoff. Welcome aboard."

Davidoff looked up and started to shout again, "What—!" but stopped, still clutching the woman to him.

"I am Captain Applebye. We are pleased to have you aboard. We'll see to it that your luggage is handled properly if you will make your way aboard, sir. It is a bit crowded here."

"Yes. Yes. I am just going," Davidoff said curtly, giving a last hug and noisy kiss.

"You will hear from me, my dear," he said, letting her go, glaring at the purser and nodding briefly to the captain as he started slowly up the gangplank.

Exchanging glances, the crowd that had been lined up behind the scene began to move up the gangplank. The woman went back to the limousine, and the captain went aboard, heading for his quarters.

Chin Ching opened the door as he approached, greeting him with a small smile and bowed head.

"Good morning, Captain."

"Good morning, Chin Ching. Everything in order here?"

"Oh, yes, Captain. Everything fine."

"Any messages?"

"Mr. Lobbyshaw, he look for you few minutes ago."

"Ah, yes. Did he say anything special?"

"Just he want to know when you coming."

"Well, you can tell him I'm here."

✳ 17 ✳

"Fresh clothes for you, Captain. And letter from Mrs. Applebye." A teapot, rolls, and fruit juice were on the desk.

"Ah, yes. Thank you. I will change."

Stripped to his skivvies, he picked up the letter and tore it open impatiently, frowning, to read her strong precise script.

My dear Samuel:

Good news! This is completely unofficial and to be kept quiet, but I have a report of the Board of Directors' meeting yesterday from Julian. You can be thankful for having such a good brother-in-law. The subject of the command of *Pacific Monarch* was on the agenda, and, after discussion of the incident of the propeller damage, it was decided that it would not count against your record and that the new command is yours if there is no further trouble. Julian did not, of course, make the motion, but I am sure his remarks were helpful in the decision. We are very happy for you, Samuel, and it will be a grand climax to your career.

The letter went on with reports of her club meetings and a charity tea she had given. He skimmed the rest, then stood deep in thought as he reread the first paragraph. With a shake of his head, he placed the letter under the blotter, and moved into the bathroom to start shaving.

There was a knock on the outer door. Robertshaw, he thought, and called "Come in" as he began lathering. "I'm in the head," he said when he heard the door open.

Robertshaw stepped inside, noticing the rumpled uniform thrown on the chair. He peered at it closely as he moved forward, looking for lipstick or powder stains. The fresh uniform was hanging on the head door.

"Good morning, Mr. Robertshaw," Sam said, face to mirror.

"Good morning, Captain. Pleasant evening ashore?"

"Yes. Yes. Fine indeed. Are we ready to sail? Any problems for me?"

Robertshaw put customs forms on the desk for the captain's signature. "Everything is in readiness, sir. There was a problem with the fuel delivery, but it's straightened out now."

"Oh. What was the trouble?"

"It seems the company was sold and the manager was released, and there was not a proper follow-up on the delivery. I remembered you knew the principals of the company and could track it down, but—since you were not here, I was able to have our agent get hold of the office and get the lighter here. They just topped off a few minutes ago."

"Well done, Robertshaw. Well done. That would have been a problem." He finished shaving, toweled his face, and came into the sitting room to put on the clean uniform. "I shouldn't like to have been delayed with this typhoon hanging around. It's not coming here, but I would like to be away on schedule."

"Indeed, sir. The tugs are alongside and all is in readiness."

"I'll be on the bridge as soon as I'm dressed," Sam said, starting to put on the fresh clothes. Chin Ching came in silently, slipped by them, and started tidying the bathroom. Robertshaw lingered for a moment as though about to say more, then turned and went out.

As Sam finished dressing, the phrases 'no further trouble' and 'climax to your career' ran through his head like a refrain.

Holden searched through the medicine cabinet until he found the paregoric and took it off the shelf. He started for the door, bottle in hand, looked down at it, and hesitated. It should be in a bag. Moving back he rummaged in a drawer until he found the right size bag. He started for the door again, then turned back to the cabinet, reached into the back for the vodka bottle, and took a quick swig.

"Paregoric. Vodka," he muttered shaking his head as he left the office. In the passageway heading for the Hong Kong Suite, he heard voices up ahead and saw a large man in a white suit about to enter the Yokohama Suite directly across from the Hong Kong Suite. The man's voice was raised in a commanding roar, directed at a room steward.

"My suitcase should be here now!" he bellowed. "Those stupid porters had no idea what I wanted." The steward stood quietly.

"Well do something, man. You do understand English, don't you, or should I use German, French or Russian? I don't know Chinese."

The steward nodded and started to leave.

"And I do not want to be disturbed. Do you understand that? Except when I call you, I don't want anyone here. Now get me my luggage." He waved his cane menacingly and the steward trotted off, head down. As Holden approached the Hong Kong door, the man glared at him as though expecting more trouble, entered his suite and then slammed the door.

I hope he doesn't need a doctor, thought Holden as he knocked on the Hong Kong door. The glow of the vodka in his gut filled him with new strength. The dark-haired woman opened the door and motioned him in without speaking. Madelaine Clare was in the same spot on the settee and seemed to be waking from a daze as she looked up at him and smiled weakly. Seeing the bag, she said, "Oh. Good. You have some."

"Yes, I do. I didn't have to go ashore."

"Hannah will take it," she said, as he stood uncertainly, then handed it to the dark-haired woman, who went into one of the staterooms.

"Be careful of it this time, dear Hannah," Madelaine called. Turning to him, she explained, "She dropped the other bottle, and she has been upset, but now it's all right. I do appreciate your bringing it. You've been most kind." She turned her smile on again.

"I—I hope you don't need it much," he said, feeling foolish. "It's not to be taken carelessly."

"Oh, yes. I know. I will be careful." She got up and followed Hannah into the cabin. Holden was about to leave when Hannah came out. He hesitated, then beckoned her toward the door. Standing in it, out of sight of the stateroom and in a low voice, he said, "As a doctor I would appreciate it if you can tell me anything I should know about Miss Clare's need for medication."

The woman gave him a long, silent stare, then spoke quietly. "Well, yes. I guess you should. I guess you know it's not for her stomach. It—it keeps her from worrying."

"Does she have problems?"

"It's her career. She was in Hong Kong to do a play at the British Theater, but it didn't go well. The reviews were not kind, and she had trouble with her lines. It's not like making a movie you know, having to remember speeches. She hasn't had any movie offers lately, and she thinks she's washed up." The woman looked on the verge of tears. "I've been with her for years, and I hate to see her like this. I broke the bottle on purpose, but I guess that wasn't smart. She really needs it."

"I'm sorry," Holden said. "I can appreciate your position. Please watch her carefully, and let me know if there is anything I can do."

* 21 *

"Thank you, sir. You can be sure and I will. You've been most kind." She gave him a small, tight smile.

"I'll keep in touch," he said as he turned down the passageway.

Sam came onto the starboard wing of the bridge, glanced at the sky, and then down at the pier. The weather had cleared slightly but there was still a threatening feel to it, and the air was heavy. It would be good to get to sea, he thought. 1150; ten minutes to sailing time, and everything looked ready. He could see the stack of the tug waiting off the port bow, and Robertshaw reported the other one in position at the port quarter. Sam gave the order to single up docklines, and Robertshaw passed it by megaphone.

On the promenade deck most of the ship's 450 passengers lined the rail, tossing paper streamers at friends on the pier, who were cheering, waving, and yelling messages in the typical gala ritual of sailing time. The ship's band, from its spot on the promenade deck above the gangplank, was blasting out "A Life on the Ocean Wave," its rhythms coming unevenly through the crowd noise. While the crew was preparing to bring the gangplank aboard, a young couple dashed from a taxi onto the gangplank and into the ship as everyone on the pier and promenade deck cheered and laughed.

At 1155 the ship's whistle gave a long, deep-throated blast that echoed off the embankment ashore, and women squealed and covered their ears. Paper streamers curled forth in renewed vigor, and the gangplank was hauled into the ship. Just as its end disappeared, a man could be seen shouldering his way toward it in a desperate rush. Sam recognized him as Martin Simms, the man who, according to Robertshaw, had just been fired from the petroleum company. Simms came to a sudden halt where the gangplank had been and glared up at the ship in angry frustration. Something odd there, Sam thought. Perhaps he'd find out next time around.

Now his problem was to get the *Monarch* cleanly away from the pier, clearing the freighter, *Cape Fear*, berthed just off his stern. The pilot would take her once he had her headed for the harbor entrance, but it was his job to get her away from the pier and turned around. The drill was to back out diagonally past the *Cape Fear* to the turning basin off to the east of the pier, where the tugs would assist in turning her around so that she had a straightaway northward shot at the narrow opening in the breakwaters that enclosed the inner harbor.

The 1800-yard Customs pier went northward from the harbor shore, which ran east-and-west, backed by the Bund and the western-style buildings of the foreign quarter on the land side of the Bund. From there, low hills rose gradually, with the main boulevard from inland sloping down the hills right to the land end of the Customs pier. Outside the breakwater that enclosed the inner harbor and the turning basin, the outer harbor, with shoals along its northwest side, led to the open waters of Tokyo Bay. There were two large ships anchored in the turning basin and many sampans and coastal freighters were clustered along the inner shore. On the opposite side of the Customs pier, the French passenger ship *Renaissance* was at the outer berth, and Sam understood that she was undergoing engine repairs. His practiced eye took in the whole panorama in preparation for bringing the *Monarch*'s great 21,000-ton bulk through it.

He checked his watch; 1158. He started to move to the wing of the bridge to give the order to cast off the last docklines, all his attention focused downwards toward the pier as he approached the rail, all his concentration on getting the ship from her berth. Suddenly there was a tremendous roar, followed by a cascading rumble—an eerie, overpowering sound he had never heard before. In the first shock, his instant reaction was that something had gone wrong with the ship's boilers, and he turned quickly to the stacks, half expecting to see a blast of steam bursting from them. Nothing had happened there, and after a moment of relief he wheeled around toward the land, where he now realized the sound had originated. An unbelievable sight stunned him as the ship shook and rocked and trembled violently.

The entire city above the shoreline was heaving in a great series of undulations like the waves of a storm at sea. Simultaneously, blocks of buildings rose and crashed, smashing open as though under a barrage of giant guns, with cloudbursts of dust shooting above them. The solid stone and brick buildings of the foreign quarter were tumbled into heaps in an instant, and down the broad boulevard descending the hill toward the pier the pavement was splitting open in an advancing arrow like the bow wave of a big ship at full speed.

The roar was overpowering, suffocating in its intensity as a great cloud of dust and smoke shot up to cover the sky. A fierce blast of hot air almost knocked him over, and a gale force wind, loaded with the smoke and dust, swept across the ship. Right behind it, the long approach causeway at the shore end of the Customs pier undulated like an agonized caterpillar, and, as he watched, a taxi making its way toward the land was thrown high in the air and fell through a gap in the road into the water. The ship was shaking violently and rolling as in a storm at sea, but unevenly, with sudden hard jolts. The shocks continued out along the pier until the shed alongside the ship was shaking and twisting, and great gaps opened and closed in the concrete decking between the shed and the ships. Among the people on the pier who had, a moment ago, been laughing and throwing back paper streamers and waving to the passengers, there was complete panic. Some were knocked off their feet; others fell right through gaps in the concrete that opened and closed in an instant, their screams barely audible above the roar of the wind.

The whole scene was blurred by the dense pall of smoke and dust. Shocks from the earthquake continued for a few more minutes, shaking the ship in uneven tremors and continuing the havoc on the pier. The bow and stern lines were still attached to the mooring bollards, but the ship had been driven several feet away from the pier after smashing against it several times during the worst tremors. Sam wondered how badly she was damaged.

It was impossible to take in all the elements of the confusion. Obviously people were being thrown to their death through the cracks on the pier; autos were being tossed and smashed like toys, and the smoke, heat, and increasing gale made everything worse. Through the murk and flying embers, Sam could see that the buildings along the Bund had all collapsed and were beginning to burst into flame.

Mikaela!

In the jumble of wrecked buildings he could not even see which had been hers, but it was gone, a pile of rubble. Would she have been there or at the consulate, just one block inland? What could have happened? Of course there was nothing he could do now—nothing, damn it.

On the bridge telephone he raised the engine room and spoke to Chief Engineer Scott.

"Mr. Scott. There is hell to pay up here. We are in a severe earthquake, and the ship has been smashed against the pier in those jolts you must have felt. Be sure that all emergency fire systems are in working order. Have someone sound the wells to see whether we are making water. She took some heavy knocks. I will let you know when we're ready to move. Right now, we can't."

"Aye, aye, sir," came Scott's thick burr. "We'll see to things."

Sam went out to the bridge wing again. The smoke and dust had become so dense that he could not even see the bow. The ship had settled back against the pier with the gale on her port bow, and some of the crewmembers had lowered rope ends and rope ladders over the side. On the pier there was fierce, brutal struggling among people trying to grab hold and be hoisted up. They were clawing and swinging punches at each other, even pulling back those who had grabbed a line. Some who were obviously injured were lying on the concrete. Sam saw Perkins climbing the ladder to the bridge, horror on his face, and went to him immediately.

"Mr. Perkins, go have the gangplank put out and bring those people on the pier aboard before they're all killed. Tell the crew to bring their ropes and ladders aboard or someone will be killed that way. Quickly!"

"Aye, aye, sir." Perkins gulped and fled back down the ladder.

The worst tremors had stopped, but there were still small aftershocks. Burning embers landing on the roof of the Customs shed soon started fires there, whipped quickly to life by the gale.

We've got to get her out of here, he thought. She'll be afire before long when that shed really gets going.

"Are the tugboats still here?" he asked Robertshaw, who had been giving orders to the firefighting crews on the decks below.

"No sir," came Robertshaw's answer in a high, tense voice. "They left."

Passengers who had been at the rail waving goodbye minutes ago were pitching in with the deck gangs to handle the hoses, which were soon wetting down the side of the ship closest to the flames ashore. The gangplank shot out of the hull and back onto the pier, and the mob on the pier made a dash for it. Sam saw Perkins and two seamen picking up those who were lying injured and carrying them aboard. Simms, too, was helping.

"What do you intend to do, Captain?" Robertshaw asked.

"We shall have to see," Sam answered. "Keep those hoses playing or we're all gone. The flames are getting worse. Blast those tugs. We can't move away by ourselves with this gale holding us in. I can't go forward. It's shoal water right ahead, and that freighter is in our way aft. Go to the stern and see if you can raise her. She'll burn too if we don't get away from here."

As he spoke, the quartermaster on watch gave a sharp cry and pointed off the port quarter. The smoke had thinned enough so that it was possible to see the bow of a large freighter charging at them out of the murk. There were Japanese characters on the bow, and *Lyons Maru* in big white letters underneath. They all stood in helpless horror, with the name looming ever larger, until the bow crashed into the *Monarch*'s port quarter with a grating, squealing crunch that could be heard above the gale. She was already backing down, with a great boil of water at the stern, so the damage was only external—but when she stopped backing and tried to move ahead again to turn for the harbor entrance, she couldn't turn against the press of the wind. Now she was headed again for the *Monarch*, near amidships.

"By God, she's going to do it this time," Sam cried. "God damn the fool—he'll split us in two!"

On came the freighter again, pushing through all sorts of debris in the water. Drifting sampans and lighters cluttered the area, some of them bumping along the *Monarch*'s side.

Just as it seemed that the freighter's bow was going to crash in sharply, a lighter loaded with burning lumber drifted between the two ships. There was a great, rending crunch as the lighter was caught between them, acting as a fender, and the burning pile of lumber scattered in the air like so many matchsticks. A man had been squatting at the outer end of a plank on the lighter as far away as possible from the flames.

"My God, look at that. That lighter's saving us but that poor sod's a goner," Sam cried, but as he spoke the lumber scattered in a fiery eruption, and the man was catapulted from the plank end onto the bow rail of the *Lyons Maru*. He clutched desperately, almost slipping off, but got a grip and was able to crawl over the rail to safety. By this time *Lyons Maru* was in full emergency reverse once more. She backed off into the gloom, disappeared, and was not seen again. She had been one of the ships at anchor in the turning basin.

If we could only get out there, Sam thought, there'll at least be more room to maneuver. One emergency gone through, but now what?

Robertshaw, sweating, and his face streaked with sooty grime, climbed the ladder on the double.

"Can't raise the freighter, Captain," he panted. "There don't seem to be many people aboard, and no one was near the bow. She had both bow anchors out, so she's really blocking us."

"We'll have to push her out of our way. We can't stay here," Sam said.

"Do you think that's wise? There will be damage." Robertshaw's voice rose with tension.

"Damage, or loss of the ship and our lives. What's your choice, Robertshaw? I'll warn Mr. Scott. Send the other mates to the fire hoses, one forward, one amidships, and alert the doctor that there will be casualties to see to. Some of those people on the pier are injured."

"We're getting refugees in from the harbor boats," Robertshaw said. "Someone opened the gangways on the port side, and people are jumping in from the sampans and lighters when they come by us."

"I'll have the gangplank back aboard as soon as everyone's clear of the pier, and then we'll have to be off."

As he spoke, he could see flame licking along the roofline of the two-story Customs shed, coming ever closer. Down on the pier Perkins and his men were staggering toward the gangplank with the limp forms of the injured.

Lying on his bunk, the doctor felt the first sudden jolts of the ship shaking and crashing against the pier, and, even deep in the ship as he was, the great roar outside shook him sharply awake. The latest shot of vodka had put him in a soft daze of semi-sleep, but he struggled off the bunk, shaking his head.

"What the hell? What the hell is this?"

He went straight to the wash basin, ran some water and splashed his face several times, then rubbed it vigorously with a towel. Something weird was happening, and he knew it would mean he was wanted. What could this be? Where was the lazy routine of a ship doctor's life? Putting on his white coat as he went, he headed out the door for sick bay.

Moving through the passageways, he was thrown against the bulkhead several times by the sudden motion of the ship. How could this be happening in port? There were explosions of some sort, and he felt a moment of panic, an urge to head for the deck and get off the ship if possible, but he fought it down and kept moving toward his office. As the jolts continued, and the roar from somewhere above him—

was it on board or outside the ship?—visions of the trenches at the front shot through his mind. Not again—Dear Lord not again. No more explosions after the months of it he had gone through. Shell shock they called it, and through the year and a half of his hospitalization, he had wondered whether he could ever practice again, much less face rows of wounded, day after day.

Another crash from above threw him sideways again, and the sound with it brought an instant flash of the night barrages at Ypres, the constant crack of shells exploding and the eerie lightning as they did.

Stewards, their narrow eyes widening in astonishment, peered out from doorways as he passed.

"What is it, Doctor? What is happening?"

"Blessed if I know; I have no idea," he answered as he stumbled forward. Few passengers were belowdecks, but in one or two cabins he could see them peering out into the passageway or trying to look out a porthole.

Through an open gangway on the port side he could see the maelstrom of smoke, dust, and flying debris hurtling by. Suddenly, through the opening a figure burst in—a coolie in torn, smeared clothes, near rags, his face streaked in dirt and blood. He staggered toward Holden, babbling in what must have been Japanese.

"Where did you come from? What is happening?" Holden shouted, but the man just jibbered and coughed and stared wildly around.

Something is on fire, Holden thought, something terrible has happened. Another jolt shook the ship. Earthquake? Could it be an earthquake? He motioned the man to follow him and went through the next passageway to the door of the sick bay.

Perkins looked down at the dirt and blood streaking his whites. The thought that Robertshaw would be after him for this flashed idiotically through his mind. All the people who could walk were already on board, but there were still some lying on the concrete and others leaning against posts or the building wall, holding themselves in pain. Some were crawling toward the gangplank. Across a fissure in the concrete a small group of women, and one man, were huddled in terror, trapped where they were. Looking down in the fissure Perkins saw several bodies caught in the pilings of the pier, their heads underwater. A man, soaking wet and blood-stained, was scrambling up the maze of pier supports, slipping back once, but still working his way upwards. A rope-end was nearby on the concrete, and Perkins dangled it down. The man grabbed for it and missed, then managed to work a foot or two higher and take hold, twisting it around his wrists. As Perkins pulled, he worked footholds up the pilings and cross-timbers until he fell gasping on the con-crete. It was Mr. Loomis, the Hong Kong pilot, who had just left the ship.

With Mr. Loomis safe, Perkins found a large plank near the building and dragged it to the fissure. Loomis stood up and helped him place it across the opening. The women still stood in panic and stared at the plank, frozen in fright and unable to move, until the man with them urged them forward. Just as they got to the plank, an aftershock made it shake, and dust fell down on them from a crack in the building wall. Looking up, Perkins could see that the roof of the building was now on fire. The women stepped back from the plank, clutching each other, but again the man urged them. Perkins moved onto the plank a few steps, holding his hand out. With their skirts swirling in the gale, one by one the women came out to him and were guided over. The man made it across just as another shock jarred the plank, and it fell into the widening fissure.

"Go aboard the ship," Perkins yelled at them above the roar of the gale and flames. "Quick! Quick!"

The two seamen who had come ashore with Perkins were guiding the last injured to the gangplank, holding them up and half dragging them. Perkins was surprised to see Mr. Simms, the man from the fuel company, carrying an injured woman in his arms. The pier now seemed clear of everyone who had been caught there. Looking toward the shore, Perkins saw that the long causeway at the land end of the pier had collapsed completely, and the roofs of a few cars and trucks were sticking up above the water at odd angles next to the ruins. No one could possibly get ashore from here. Beyond, through the thinning smoke, the town was a smoking, flaming heap of wreckage, barely glimpsed in the gloom. The gale had blown the first great cloud of dust from the beginning of the earthquake on out over the harbor, and the smoke from the buildings on fire came in uneven swirls. The acrid stench of fire, dust, and old buildings suddenly disemboweled was almost painful in its bitterness.

He knew that the ship would be in real danger if she couldn't leave the pier. At least the gangplank should be back on board, he thought, now that the pier seemed deserted. Over his head the flames on the roof were fanning higher and making their way out closer to the ship. Soon the *Monarch* would be in flames herself if she couldn't move.

It was time to be aboard, but he decided to make one last check of the area in case any injured had not been picked up. All seemed clear, and he was turning to board the gangplank when his eye caught a slight movement in an alcove of the building that was partially out of the wind— just a little flicker of cloth. As he rounded the corner of the alcove, there, huddled down together were two small children. A blond boy was holding a smaller tow-headed figure in his arms, and his eyes turned up in wide-eyed fright when Perkins appeared. The smaller figure, a girl, was crying and sobbing.

"Come with me, children; quickly, come with me to the ship. There'll be fire here very soon," he called.

The children, perhaps six and four years old, scrambled up, and he took each by the hand.

"Are you alone? Were you with someone?"

"Our mother and father," the boy said, "but they're gone."

"Gone?"

"There," the boy said, pointing at the fissure. "They fell."

Oh, God, thought Perkins. The bodies I saw down there. There had been a man and a woman.

"Can you help them?" the girl asked through her tears.

"There's no way. I'm sorry. There's no way."

The children hung back against the pull of his hands, staring at the fissure. Just then, a small shock jarred the pier and the building. A burning piece of the roof fell to the concrete just across the fissure, then caromed into the opening in a shower of sparks. The girl screamed, and the boy stared in horror.

"Come now; we must!" Perkins pulled them along. "We can't stay here another minute."

With the children staring back over their shoulders at the opening, where a spurt of smoke and sparks was shooting up, he pulled them to the gangplank and into the ship. A burst of flame on the roof was greeted by a cascade of water from the ship's firehoses, drenching the pier where they had just been in a great splatter of water and steam, while hoses playing on the side of the ship sent water streaming down over the gangplank.

There was a crush of dazed people from the pier in the

reception area. Many were bleeding and streaked with dirt, and some were prone on the deck. Stratford, the head purser, was circulating among them, trying to direct them up the stairway to the main lounge two decks up, and there was gradually a stumbling movement to follow his directions. Through the open gangway on the port side of the reception area bedraggled coolies, soaking wet, some in burnt rags, staggered into the hall, wild-eyed and confused, coming from small boats and rafts that were banging along the *Monarch*'s hull.

The children, their eyes wide, clung fiercely to Perkins' hands, and he wondered what he could do with them. He should get back on deck, but he couldn't just leave them, lost and terrified as they were. The boy winced whenever Perkins pulled hard on his arm.

"Do you know someone on board?" he asked the boy. "Were you saying goodbye to someone?"

"I—I—" the boy struggled to control himself, tears welling in his eyes. "Daddy was delivering some papers to a man he worked for. He and Mummy brought us with them to see the ship, and then we were going to the beach."

"Do you know the man? Did you see him? Do you remember his name?"

"Mister—Mister—I think it was David something. He's a big man in a white suit."

"David? Do you remember his last name?"

"That was it, only longer."

Perkins went to the purser's desk and found a copy of the passenger list. "Damon, Darwin—Davidoff. Is that it? Davidoff?"

The boy nodded uncertainly. "I guess so," he murmured.

"Yokohama Suite," Perkins read. "Come on, children. We'll take you to his cabin, and he can take care of you. I have to go away for a while. What are your names?"

"Bridgeman, sir. Peter and Susan."

Pushing through the throng on the stairway, not waiting for the elevator, he led them upward to the boat deck, where the suites were located, and along the passageway to the Yokohama Suite door. He knocked on it loudly.

There was no answer for a moment, then from behind the closed door a muffled growl, "I said I don't want to be disturbed. What is it?"

"Mr. Davidoff? Please open. It's important." Perkins said.

"Who is it?"

"Fourth Mate Perkins, sir. I must see you."

"I have no business with you."

"This is important. Please open up, sir."

The door opened a crack, and Davidoff glared through the slit.

"What do you want? What is happening to the ship? We should be sailing. What is all the noise and smoke?"

"There's been an earthquake. There are some children here named Bridgeman. I believe their father works for you. He and his wife are missing on the pier, and I need to leave the children with you for safekeeping. I have other duties I must get to quickly."

"I don't want them here. Take them away."

"But, sir—" The door slammed loudly.

As Perkins stood in bewilderment, the Hong Kong door opened and a stocky, dark-haired woman looked out. Peering out behind her was a woman Perkins recognized as Madelaine Clare, the movie actress.

"What has happened?" asked the first woman. "What is all the noise and confusion? Are we in danger?"

"There has been an earthquake. Very serious. I—these children were with their parents on the pier saying goodbye to the man in this suite and their parents are...missing. I was hoping he would take them in for now, but—" he pointed to the closed door.

"Oh, dear." Madelaine Clare came closer, standing next to Hannah, and looked down at Peter and Susan. "Oh, the poor dears," she cried. "They're all alone?"

"I'm afraid so. Mr. Davidoff doesn't seem to know them. He refused to take them in."

Peter and Susan, holding hands tightly, looked up, wide-eyed and shaking. Peter was barely controlling tears, but Susan's eyes filled with them, and she gave small, snuffling sobs.

"How awful," Madelaine said. "We—we can take them here if there is nowhere else. We have plenty of room. Come here, dears. Come on into our cabin. Hannah and I will take care of you."

"That's awfully good of you, Miss Clare," Perkins said. "I must get to the bridge right away, but I didn't want to leave them alone. Their names are Peter and Susan, Peter and Susan Bridgeman. My name is Charles Perkins, fourth mate. I will check with you when things calm down, but we must get the ship underway. I must go."

"Well, we'll do what we can," Madelaine said. "Come children." She held out a hand and smiled. For a moment, they didn't move, looking up at Perkins, then slowly and hesitantly started through the door. Once inside, Peter turned, drew himself up and spoke to Perkins.

"Thank you very much, sir. Susan and I thank you."

Perkins reached out a hand to pat him on the head, hesitated and gripped him by the shoulder instead.

"Take care," he said, and turned to go to the bridge.

The captain and Robertshaw, on the starboard wing of the bridge, had watched as the refugees came aboard.

"That seems to be all, Captain," Robertshaw said. They saw Perkins leading the children aboard.

As he spoke, Loomis, the Hong Kong pilot, staggered onto the bridge, his wet clothes covered with blood and slime from the pilings of the pier.

"Good God, Mr. Loomis," Sam cried. "Were you down there?"

"Indeed, Captain. I was thrown down into the water when the pier opened up, with several other people. Some of them were crushed between the pilings while they were moving. Oh, God—" he faltered and shook his head. "The whole place was shaking and twisting, but I landed in the water without being caught in the pilings. When they stopped shaking I started to climb up, and your mate was there with a rope when I got near the top. Saved my life, he did. Never could have made it up there by myself."

"You're all bloody. Do you need help?"

"I'm all right. Just scratches and cuts from the barnacles on the pilings, I think. Can I help you here?"

"We're in a fix. Can't go ahead into shoal water and can't move off the pier without tugs in this blasted gale. That freighter astern of us has us blocked there, but we'll all fry here if we don't get out soon. We've got to get that ship to move."

Just then, Perkins burst into the bridge and came to a halt next to the group, wild-eyed and breathing hard.

"Well done, Perkins," Sam said. "All secure on the pier?"

"Yes, sir, nobody left. Oh, Mr. Loomis—"

"Thanks to you lad, I'm here. I think I'm the only one who got out from that bloody crack."

Sam turned to Loomis again. "We've been trying to raise the *Cape Fear* by wireless but they don't answer, and we can't get anyone's attention from our stern. We'll have to

✳ 37 ✳

send someone, to hail them from the pier, if it's possible."
He looked at Robertshaw.

Robertshaw's eyes opened wide. "Perhaps the stern
again. Someone..."

"I'll go, Captain," Perkins offered. "I'm familiar with
the cracks down there. I think I can make it."

"Good lad. On your way, and hurry. Tell them we both
must move right away or we'll both be on fire. Don't take no
for an answer!"

Perkins fled off the bridge.

"I'll have to have a look off the stern," Sam said. "If she
doesn't move, we'll have to do something. Catch your breath
for a moment, Mr. Loomis. You've had a bad shaking. Then
we'll see what's to be done."

"Where's the Yokohama pilot?" Loomis asked Robertshaw
as the captain went down the bridge ladder.

"His launch was alongside ready to put him aboard
when we got to the turning basin, but I'm sure he left. I
haven't seen him."

Sam started down the starboard promenade deck, but it
was so blocked with crews working the hoses that he turned
off through the smoking room to the port side. As he came
out the door to the deck, he could see the shoreline through
the smoke, now less clouded with dust after the first great
blast from the original collapse of the buildings, and the
sight of what must have been Mikaela's building lying in
rubble stabbed him with a jolt of physical fear. Could she
possibly have survived? God, if he could only do something!
His eyes were burning from the smoke and hot blasts of
wind, and he felt an extra sting in them at the thought of
what might have happened.

Hurrying along the deck, he could see over the side that
small boats were coming up to the open gangways, with
people leaping aboard from them. There were even swimmers
in the water crying to be taken aboard. Some crewmembers

were there with rope ladders. What a mess it would be below. What could be done with all these people? As he reached midships, he noticed a Chinese deck steward methodically folding steamer rugs and placing them on deck chairs.

"Why are you bothering with that?" Sam asked him incredulously.

"My job, Captain. My job." The man bobbed his head. "No one tell me no."

"Well, those rugs will be needed down at the main saloon. Lots of injured people coming aboard. Take them down there."

"Aye, sir. Aye, sir. I do."

Moving along quickly, Sam couldn't help an amused grunt at the thought of the steward carefully doing his job with all hell breaking loose. Amazing Chinese. Amazing.

Out on the fantail at the stern, he could see that the *Cape Fear* was standing well away from the pier; the flames from the burning shed were not a direct threat to her yet. Both her starboard and port anchor chains were tending out, as she had evidently dropped both anchors. In the 100 or so feet between the *Monarch*'s stern and the *Cape Fear*'s bow there was a mass of floating debris—wrecked lighters and sampans half-awash, with loose lumber all over. Could the screws and rudder take it? It would be a miracle not to have them hopelessly fouled.

There was one positive thought. The *Monarch* had been built in Germany but never commissioned during the war. She had come to Great Britain, and eventually to the C & O, as war reparations, and she had an unusual propulsion system. Instead of the standard gearing for propeller shafts, she had a newly invented hydraulic system, a German innovation, tried out on her for the first time. It was supposed to have a flexibility that could withstand shocks better than the conventional system. Well, this would be a test.

Looking over the freighter's bow, he could see no sign of life there. Farther aft, by the midships house, hoses were playing over the port side against a burning barge that was jammed against the ship, but there was no way he could get anyone's attention. He turned to look at the Customs shed and saw that the flames were growing higher despite the play from the *Monarch*'s hoses. Down on the pier a figure in white uniform zig-zagged through the wreckage, and he realized it was Perkins on his way back. Looking up, Perkins saw him and made a helpless negative shrug.

Blast. The decision hit him in the pit of his stomach. There was nothing for it but to smash their way out, taking the freighter with them. Every instinct cringed at the thought of the collision, but it was the only way to save the ship. He had to do it, he decided, as he swung around and hurried back toward the bridge. If only the tugboats were still there it would be much simpler.

He decided to take the starboard promenade deck despite the confusion of the hoses. He wanted a better idea of how the fire was doing, and of the work of the crew. First Mate Barclay had one group of Chinese deck-hands amidships, with several passengers helping to bring the hoses forward to a new spot. He also spotted the violinist and saxophone player from the ship's orchestra pitching in.

"It's a losing battle, Captain," Barclay shouted to him as he came near. "The fire's too big now for the hoses to reach all of it. We're keeping the ship wet down, but I don't know how long that will be any good."

"Keep it up," Sam said. "We're going to get out of here somehow as soon as possible. You'll hear the whistle."

At the next hose crew, Simms, his shirt torn and

bloodied, was one of the volunteers. Sam stopped next to him for a moment. "Thank God you're safe, Mr. Simms. Sorry about the news of your company. Surprised to see you here."

"A bloody mess, Captain—a bloody mess. Lucky you put the gangplank out again or we'd all have been goners on the pier. Lots of bad injuries."

"Yes, I'm sure. Thank you for helping here. We've got to get underway somehow," he called over his shoulder as he continued on toward the bridge, threading his way through the welter of hoses and struggling crewmen. The heat was intense despite the cascades of water from the hoses, and the flames could be seen spreading along the shed roof just beyond the ship's rail.

He and Perkins arrived at the bridge ladder at the same time, and Perkins, breathlessly dishevelled, gave a quick report that he had not been able to raise anyone on *Cape Fear*.

"There are very few people aboard, Captain," he reported, "and they are all on the port side."

"We'll have to smash our way through, then," Sam said, feeling sick as he said it. "Mr. Robertshaw, pass the word to cut the bow and stern lines as soon as we are ready to get underway." He went to the engine room telephone and signalled for Mr. Scott. "Are we ready for full speed astern?" he called, and the answer came back affirmative. "Free the lines, Mr. Robertshaw," he ordered. As soon as the dock lines were severed by men with axes, he stepped to the engine telegraph, signalled for full speed astern, and ordered the emergency reverse signal of four blasts on the ship's whistle.

The gale was still strong on the port bow, but the smoke had thinned more, and there was not as much dust in the air. He watched the pier to see how soon the ship gathered way, feeling the powerful boil of the propellers aft at full speed astern. He wanted to duck his head and not watch as the *Monarch*'s stern, moving ever more rapidly, closed with the *Cape Fear*'s bow. A sick feeling stabbed his stomach while he waited for the crash of steel on steel. Overhead, the ship's whistle, giving short blasts, blended with the roar of the wind in a howling crescendo, a nightmare wail of desperation that added to the wild fear that filled him.

He expected the center of *Monarch*'s stern to crash into the high, threatening knife of the freighter's bow, but, at the last minute, the stern sheered off to port. The pile of wreckage between the ships must have acted as a buffer, and the big ship's starboard quarter slid along the freighter's bow, cringing and crashing, but continuing to move, and he could see that *Cape Fear* was being carried along by the force of the *Monarch*'s backward charge. Even above the wind's howl and the roar of the ships' whistle, he could hear the rending screech of steel against steel.

Monarch's bow was now a good sixty feet away from the pier, and the ships had moved out beyond the end of the two-story shed. The wind was taking the flames, smoke, and sparks diagonally away from them, but the heat was still intense, and it looked as though the ship's motorboat, hanging from davits off the starboard bow, might still catch fire. Looking aft, Sam saw that several coastal freighters were right in the path of the sternward push of the two big ships, and he called for "All Stop" on the engine telegraph. No time to tangle with any more wreckage. Meanwhile, First Mate Barclay and a hose crew had gone into the forward well deck and were playing water on the motorboat, whose paint had begun to scorch and smoke. Sam marveled at how they could stand the heat, as it was fiercely hot even on the bridge. Probably the fact that they were all soaking wet, their shirts plastered to them as they played the hoses, made the difference, but he felt for them.

The aftward momentum of the two ships continued and was carrying them quite close to the craft astern. Sam felt that the propellers must have cleared *Cape Fear*'s anchor lines by now, and he telegraphed for a quick burst ahead on the port screw to stop her way and kick the stern further out. Just after it took hold, he felt a hard jolt and realized by the lack of turbulence under the port quarter that the screw had fouled. Cursing, he frantically signalled "All Stop" again. It was the freighter's port cable, no doubt.

There the ships were, locked in a strange embrace and immobilized. At least they were far enough off the pier to keep the flames under control by playing hoses from the bow. It was now an hour and a half since the first great shock of the earthquake, and the fire on the shed seemed to have passed its peak under the constant play of the ship's hoses. On the other side of the ship, burning lighters and sampans continued to be blown against the hull by the gale, and hoses on that side were played on them to keep the flames from spreading to the ship. On some, crewmembers would suddenly be caught, disappearing in a burst of flames and their screams could be heard over the wind's roar. Others, luckier, were able to jump from their potential funeral pyres into open gangways in the ship's hull. Everywhere in the harbor, flaming wreckage was being driven before the wind, and fires were still burning in some of the buildings on shore. Preoccupied as he was with saving his ship, Sam was just beginning to realize the scope of the disaster, the complete wreckage of everything within sight and God knew how much farther inland. Under all the anxiety over the ship's peril, the thought of Mikaela, a desperate desire to know what might have happened to her, stung him, and he also began to realize that the Yokohama office of C & O, the various consulates, the restaurants and hotels he knew so well, were no doubt in ruins. How many dead? It was almost too much to grasp. He forced himself back to the immediate situation of the ship, and the more than a thousand lives that depended on his actions. There was no time now to check below for what was happening to the passengers, or the people who had come on board from the pier, or the refugees from the harbor. There was nothing he could do to move the ships at the moment. He wondered if he could even make sure that the pier fire did not spread to them. Through his burning, stinging eyes, he watched the work of the hose crews.

Dr. Holden finished putting ointment on the burns of the coolie who had followed him to sick bay, and the man stood uncertainly, not knowing what to do. Holden showed him out the door and was surprised to see that there was a queue of people in the passageway. There were Europeans in smeared, torn Western clothes, coolies in their work clothes, and some people barely covered by rags. An assistant purser was bringing more people as he looked. Spying Holden, the purser came forward.

"Mr. Stratford told me to bring these people here, Doctor, but I didn't expect so many. There are lots of people hurt who can't move. It's terrible—terrible."

Holden's eyes ranged along the queue with dismay. This was an emergency beyond belief. How could he ever treat them all? Would he have enough supplies? He could see that most of them were bleeding or burned, and there was a low murmur of moans and sobbing.

"I'll need help," he said to the purser. "Tell Mr. Stratford to find any doctors and nurses among the passengers who can give a hand and ask them to come down here. Are we underway?"

"Not yet. We're alongside the pier and it's burning.

Most of these people were on the pier seeing friends off. A lot of them must have been killed."

"Oh, God. Oh, God," Holden groaned. "There'll be more, I'm sure. I'll do what I can here, but see if you can get help."

Before he could bring the next person in the line into the office, Holden saw Madelaine Clare's companion, Hannah, hurrying toward him and looking in amazement at the queue of injured.

"Doctor," she gasped, "I had no idea of what was happening. All these people."

"Did you want something?"

"There is a little boy who was brought to our cabin and he has an injured arm. I was going to ask if you could come see him, but—" She looked around at the waiting people.

"As you can see," he said, "things are in a state here. These people were caught on the pier when the quake hit, and more are coming in from boats in the harbor. I'm going to do what I can here. Can you bring him down?"

"Oh yes, I will. I didn't know." She turned and hurried away, and he went back to work. The cries and moans of the people in the passageway followed him inside his office, and he could hear the roaring noise from topsides, though the ship was no longer shaking with the aftershocks. Then, suddenly, there was a sense of motion and the distant blasts of the whistle. There were lurches and crashes, a hard jolt, and the motion stopped.

The urge to go on deck and somehow escape grabbed at his insides. What would be the use of all this if the ship caught fire? He wished he knew more about what was going on. How the hell could he handle that mob of moaning people outside and Lord knew how many more in other parts of the ship? Hands shaking, he reached into the cabinet for the vodka bottle, and the fire in his throat and gut from the quick swig gave him an immediate jolt that calmed his nerves. Just as he put the bottle back, Chief Purser Stratford, strain and anxiety showing through his usual haughty imperturbability, came to the door.

"We have a frightful crisis, Doctor," he said. "There are wounded people all over this ship, and more coming aboard from small boats in the harbor."

"So I gather," Holden answered. "I asked your assistant to see if there are doctors and nurses among the passengers who can help me."

"Yes. We're looking. But I don't see how you can handle it here. We'll have to set up a bigger headquarters for you."

"One of the lounges?"

"Possibly, but they're so crowded with people who aren't hurt, and our passengers too. Everyone is close to panic." He paused, breathing heavily and shaking his head. "How are your supplies? Can you handle all this?"

"I'll be short on burn ointment if there are too many. I have a pretty good supply of bandages. Morphine, I don't know. Perhaps enough for the worst cases of pain. Could you get the stewards to make a lot of tea? I can use that for burns when I run out of tannic."

"I'll see to that. Yes," Stratford said.

"How about the suites?" Holden asked. "They're big enough, and it wouldn't disturb the rest of the people."

"An idea, yes, an idea. We'd have to move the passengers from them. I don't know how Miss Clare will react, and that Davidoff—" he shook his head.

"No harm in trying. I am cramped here."

A new sense of panic threatened to take over, but Holden took a deep breath and steadied himself just as

Hannah appeared at the door. She looked at the two men uncertainly.

"Oh, Doctor. I'm sorry. I—I—it's just that the little boy won't leave his sister. She's so terribly frightened, and he's being very brave. Says he'll be all right. I don't know whether—" her voice trailed off.

The men exchanged glances and Holden spoke to her as calmly as possible. "We may be up there soon, anyway. We may have to take over the suites as emergency hospital space. I hope Miss Clare will understand."

"Oh," Hannah looked shocked. "Well, yes. If it's necessary, we'll help, of course. I'll go tell her."

"We'll let you know soon," Stratford put in. "We hate to inconvenience Miss Clare, but this is a very real emergency."

"Yes. Of course. Yes." Hannah hurried away.

"We had better do it," Stratford said. "I think that's the best arrangement. How about your supplies? We'll have to move them."

"They're all in these three cabinets and on the shelves in that locker. If you can have the cabinets moved, the stuff on the shelves can be put in boxes. Give me a couple of hands, and we can manage. It'll be easier to work with other doctors or nurses in a bigger space." Holden gave a distraught look around the cabin, calculating what would have to be done.

"I'll send some men right away," Stratford said.

"Keep looking for volunteers, doctors and nurses, and send them up there, please," Holden went on. "And if I run out of bandages, we'll have to use sheets and towels, if you can do that. These people outside will have to go up there too. How's the ship doing, by the way? Are we going to survive?"

"There's a terrible danger, I'd say," Stratford gave an involuntary shudder. "I hope the captain can save us, but we're in an awful spot. I haven't been topsides lately, but I think we've moved from the pier with that last lurching and smashing. God only knows." He turned and left.

On the bridge, Sam watched the flames roaring through the Customs shed and noted that the wind had backed more off the port bow, taking the smoke and flames away from the ship at a better angle, and wind strength seemed to be abating. The *Monarch* was held fast by her entanglement with the *Cape Fear*, and the freighter's anchors were holding both ships now. For the moment, there was nothing more he could do, and a feeling of helplessness came over him. They were safe for now, but there would still be tremendous problems in getting her away from the harbor with all the burning wreckage and derelict lighters and sampans clogging the area. Still something would have to be done. He passed his hand over his forehead and burning eyes and noticed that Robertshaw was watching him closely.

"Any orders, Captain?" Robertshaw asked.

"For the moment, no. Not much we can do right now except keep the flames away. Keep an eye on things. I've got to go to the head."

He went into his quarters and used the toilet, realizing that he had not been to it since early morning, and also had not eaten. As he came out into the sitting room, Chin Ching materialized with a sandwich and a pot of tea on a tray and put it on the desk.

"You eat, maybe?" he said, with a small bow.

"Ah, Chin Ching, yes. Thank you. I guess I can grab a bite," and he picked up the sandwich quickly.

"Things very bad, Captain."

"Yes, terrible, terrible." As he stood by the desk, eating rapidly, he looked down and saw Alicia's letter beside the tray. Chin Ching must have turned it up in dusting the desk. Again the phrase "no further trouble" ran through his mind, and he gave a snort of irony. "No further trouble—just an earthquake and typhoon winds!" Chin Ching had poured a cup of tea, and its spicy heat was a bracer.

The steward looked at him and said. "Your eyes red, Captain. They hurt you?"

"Yes, it's the blasted smoke and dust out there."

"I make something to fix."

"Good. Good, but later. I must be on the bridge now."

Robertshaw was on the wing watching the flames.

"Any change, Robertshaw?"

"The wind is less, I think. And it's keeping the flames away."

"Thank God for small favors." Sam checked over the scene. The whole shed was now engulfed in flames, but the fires on the Bund had lessened. He searched the tumble of ruins to try to figure out what had happened to Mikaela's building. The whole area was one big jumble of wreckage, with a few smoldering fires sending up smoke. Farther inland there were many pillars of smoke as far as the eye could see, rising up more directly in the lessening breeze. He shuddered and groaned inwardly. It looked hopeless.

"Call the mates here, Mr. Robertshaw," Sam ordered. "Mr. Scott and Mr. Stratford too. We'll have to go over things, take stock and make some plans."

"How do you plan to get us out of here?" Robertshaw asked, his eyes narrow.

"A very good question. There's nothing that can be done just now, but we'll have to work it out somehow. After we talk, we'll have to do something about the freighter."

One by one, the mates and Mr. Scott arrived on the

bridge wing. Just as the last man appeared and they started to go into the bridge itself there was a tremendous, roaring crash on the pier. All turned startled glances to the sound, and the big two-story shed collapsed into a smoldering heap, sparks shooting high above it. Flickers of flame rose here and there, and smoke filled the air, swirling off to leeward. The ship's hoses played a long stream on it from the bow, with hisses of steam rising where the water splashed. Still the glow of heat beat on them fiercely. Nobody said anything for a moment as they all continued to stare at the ruins.

"Well, that's one less worry," Sam broke the silence. "We'll be safer here for now while we untangle things."

They gathered inside, and he faced them, aware of the anxious strain on their faces.

"I don't have to tell you how serious this situation is," he started. "We've got an enormous task ahead of us to save the ship and all our people, as well as the refugees.

"Before we talk about other problems, I want to know about the refugees, and how we are handling all that, Mr. Stratford."

"It's a mess, Captain, a mess," Stratford blurted, "but we are doing our best. The doctor and I decided to take over the suites as an emergency station. There's no room in the regular doctor's office for the mob we have aboard. Many burns, broken bones, cuts and bruises. We're transferring his gear up to the suites now, and we're looking for doctors and nurses among the passengers to volunteer help. As for food, we'll be feeding everybody in cafeteria style in the second-class dining room except the first-class passengers, but we may have to take over their dining room too if we get more crowded. People are coming aboard all the time from boats in the harbor."

"We must do everything we can," the captain said. "Have the passengers in the suites been told?"

"We told Miss Clare, but not the others yet."

"It may be sticky, but we'll have to do it."

"Perkins has already had a problem with Davidoff," Stratford said.

Sam turned to Perkins. "What was that?" he asked.

"There are two children who were seeing him off with their parents. I think the father worked for him. The parents are missing on the pier, so I brought the children to him as the only person they knew on board, but he wouldn't let them in. Miss Clare has them."

"He's a nasty chap, I've heard. Needs kid glove treatment. Well, he'll have to cooperate. Now, Perkins, I want you to take the motor lifeboat and get a line onto the pier when the fire dies down enough. I don't like our just hanging on the freighter's anchors."

"Aye, aye, sir," Perkins gulped, his eyes popping, a stab of fear in his gut.

"After that, you are to check around the harbor and the waterfront for any survivors you can rescue. There must be hundreds of people in trouble right along the shore here."

"Can we manage any more refugees?" Robertshaw asked.

"We will have to, Mr. Robertshaw. We must do what we can."

When Perkins left, the captain went over the assignments of the other officers, who were to continue to supervise firehoses, check for hull and engineering damage, and assist Stratford in organizing medical help. As they hurried off to their duties, the thought came home to him that all this would be useless if he couldn't get the ship safely away. He sighed and headed out to the bridge wing again, glancing once more at the wrecked houses along the Bund. Oh God. If he could only do something. Something.

And that phrase "no more trouble" ran through his brain like a refrain.

With it came involuntary memories from years past, of his first berth as a cabin boy on his grandfather's sailing ship; of the nasty seas, chills, and boredom of the North Sea; of the brutal cold, mud, and squalor of the gold fields and the look in Jack Pearson's eye as he lay dying. There was the first storm at sea in his first command, when he brought her through the terrifying ordeal, and the years of progress with C & O; and the typhoon in Hong Kong, when the failure of Perkins to carry out his task brought back an awareness of his own fear of failure in his early assignments. Shaking himself with a conscious effort and focusing on the dying fires of the Customs shed, he forced the memories out of his thoughts. Now. Now. Now. Nothing else mattered but now, and getting the *Monarch* safely away.

Stratford and Holden climbed the boat deck and began knocking on the doors of the suites. The Americans in the Honolulu Suite and the British in the Vancouver Suite agreed to cooperate and move to smaller cabins that were vacant. Madelaine Clare met them at the door to the Hong Kong Suite and asked them in.

"I'm glad you're here, Doctor." She turned her large eyes up at him, close to tears. "The little boy is in pain, I know, but he won't say so. The darling little girl is so terrified. Can you help him?"

"Yes, I'll try," Holden answered, "but we really came to ask you to let us use this suite as an infirmary. There are many injured people aboard, and we have a real emergency. We must have space to take care of them."

"Oh, yes, anything," she cried. "Hannah and I can help you. Please tell us what to do."

"First let me look at the boy," Holden said. "I'll do what I can."

Madelaine went to the cabin off the sitting room and brought Peter out, holding his right hand. His left arm hung limply at his side. Biting his lip, tear-filled eyes looking up at Holden, he drew himself up to attention.

"This is the doctor, Peter," Madelaine said softly.

"Let me look," Holden said, carefully unbuttoning Peter's jacket and shirt. "Does it hurt, Peter?"

"Yes, sir," Peter nodded, his eyes becoming more tearful.

"Why, it's dislocated," Holden said. "I can fix it, Peter, but this is going to hurt when I do it. Brave boy, now. Are you ready?"

Peter nodded silently, and Holden gave a sharp pull and a twist as Peter let out a shrill little cry, then bit his lip fiercely.

"There now. Can you move it?" Holden asked.

Peter gave his arm a tentative shake and swung it a little. A sudden smile lit his face. "Yes, sir. Yes, sir, I can," he said in a small voice.

"Good. It will be sore, but it should be better soon. Do you have any other sore places or cuts?"

"No, sir. I'm all right now," Peter answered.

Madelaine hugged Peter to her and smiled down at him. "There, Peter. Isn't that wonderful." Turning to Holden, she asked, "What do you want us to do? I want to help, but I hope the children can stay with me. They have no one else."

"You can still use the bedrooms, Miss Clare," Stratford said. "We'll just use the sitting room, and if you and your companion can help us, we'll be most grateful. We will use all the suites and the corridor as an emergency station."

"What is happening outside?" Madelaine asked. "It seems so terrible. Is the ship all right?"

"Yes. For now. We are away from the fire on the pier,

and we'll be here for a while. It's been a frightful disaster. The whole town is in ruins. We're doing our best to help survivors. We'll be back here soon to set up the emergency station. Please wait. It's very kind of you. We need all the help we can get."

Stratford turned to leave, and Holden put out his hand to Madelaine's arm and gripped it firmly. "Thank you very much," he said. "You're wonderful to help. Take care till we come back."

They crossed the passageway and knocked on the door to the Yokohama Suite. At first there was no answer, but finally, after repeated sharp raps on the door, there came a growling answer from behind it. "Who is it?"

"This is the chief purser, Mr. Davidoff."

"I have no business with you."

"This is very important. We must talk to you."

"Go away."

"I repeat, sir. We must talk to you. This is an emergency. Please open the door."

"Leave me alone and go away."

"These are captain's orders, sir. You must open the door."

"Why isn't the ship sailing? We should be away from here."

"There is an emergency, sir. A bad earthquake. We must use your quarters as an emergency hospital."

"No."

"I repeat, sir. This is an order from the captain."

"I have paid for this suite and I am staying in it. Go away."

"We will be back with a master key to open your door, sir. It would be much better if you would cooperate."

"You can't come in. I'm staying here."

"We will be back, Mr. Davidoff. You have no choice but to cooperate."

With a helpless shrug to Holden, Stratford turned away. "We'll have to report to the captain. This man has no choice."

"He's a nasty one," Holden said. "It's going to be trouble."

"We shall see," Stratford said as they made their way down the passageway.

With the meeting over and the mates off to their duties, Sam turned his eye on the ruins of the shed. The flames were all out now, and the heat was less. The breeze had fallen off almost to a calm. The motor lifeboat came under the bow, took a dock line, and headed for the pier. One of the seamen scrambled quickly onto the bulkhead and put the eye of the line over a bollard. He moved rapidly back to the boat, jumping in, and just as he did, an aftershock hit the pier, making it shake.

"Good God. No more, no more," Sam muttered to himself, but it was a small shock with no follow-up. He turned his binoculars to the shorefront, where Perkins was now heading with the lifeboat. He could see people standing in the water along the shoreline.

The ships were secure for now, but he had to plan ahead. With twilight approaching, and all the wreckage around the two ships and farther out in the turning basin, it would be impossible to try to move now. As long as no fire threatened, they would have to wait out the night and try to move in the morning. It was a frightening prospect. There was no telling when fires on shore would spread more, and the surface of the harbor was coated with oil from storage tanks that had collapsed. He decided that he had to find out more about the *Cape Fear*. Now that she was alongside he should be able to find someone on board to talk to.

Robertshaw was slumped in a chair by the navigation

table in the bridge, his eyes closed and his head nodding. Sam spoke to him quietly. "I'm going back to the stern to check on the freighter, Mr. Robertshaw. Please keep an eye out here."

Robertshaw shook himself and stood up slowly.

As Sam went aft on the starboard promenade deck, there was not the confusion there had been when the fires were alongside. Seamen, their clothes plastered wetly to them, still stood by the hoses, but none of them was working at the moment. Two thirds of the way aft, he came to the bow of the *Cape Fear* another deck down. Her bridge and superstructure were just at the fantail of the *Monarch*. Some of the *Monarch*'s railing was bent and twisted where the ships had scraped together, and *Cape Fear*'s well-deck bulkhead was pushed in. There were scars and streaks of bare metal along her hull, but none of the damage appeared to be too serious.

Sam leaned over the rail at the fantail and saw a figure standing on the *Cape Fear*'s deck.

"Ahoy there," he called. "Aboard the *Cape Fear*."

The man came forward uncertainly.

"I am captain of this ship," Sam called. "I would like to speak to your captain."

The man looked at him dumbly and shook his head. He was not an Oriental, but he obviously didn't speak English.

"Captain—Cap-i-tan—Cap-i-tan," Sam enunciated and the man moved away. Soon another figure appeared.

"Yes sir. May I help you?" He spoke with a Scandinavian accent.

"Yes. I am the captain of this ship, and I would like to speak to your captain. We must work together here."

"We have no captain. Dead. All officers dead on shore."

"Who is in charge?" Sam asked.

"I am bosun mate. I run crew now."

"Can anyone handle the ship? We will have to move from here as soon as possible tomorrow."

"Not so good. Maybe you help us."

"Have you engineers?"

"Yes. We have some black gang."

"I'm sorry about your officers. This has been a terrible thing. Were they all on shore?"

"All but second mate. He went ashore with two men to find captain at ship's office and he was killed in the fire. One man got back here."

"Good God! I'm sorry. We'll have to see what we can do. Will you please take lines from us so we are secure for the night and keep a man on watch here who speaks English so we can plan. My port screw is fouled on your port anchor cable. We'll have to work together. I'll get back to you when we can. What is your name, sir?"

"Christiansen, sir. Eric Christiansen."

"Thank you, Mr. Christiansen. We will keep in touch with you."

Taking the port deck back to the bridge, he saw that there was a hose crew still active there, tending to fires of burning boats and wreckage that came alongside the hull.

As the lifeboat neared the shoreline, Perkins could see that there were many people along the water's edge. The smell of the wrecked and burned buildings grew stronger the closer they came and he heard cries and yells from the shore. There was wreckage on the beach, and a film of oil subdued the chop in the harbor to low mounds, shining slickly. The boat's bow wave and wake turned a dirty brown when they plowed through it. He was not sure of the depth, but, as he came close, people began wading toward the boat, crying out. The keel edged onto the bottom, and the waders were alongside grappling at the rail and climbing over it. All were oil-covered, and some were almost naked. Their eyes and teeth stood out whitely in their smeared faces. Some were Europeans and some were Japanese, but in the condition they were in it was hard to tell which.

"Easy, easy!" he cried, afraid they would swamp the boat. His two Chinese crewmen stood by the rail, helping people aboard and controlling the rush. In no time the boat was full of a sodden, smeared crowd of people, gasping, gurgling and retching, with more coming toward them from the beach. When the absolute limit was reached, he backed off, leaving figures in the water, their arms raised imploringly.

"Later," he called. "Back later."

The boat, very low in water, lurched and wallowed as he turned for the ship, and he thought for a moment it might capsize.

Near him, a man in the remains of a business suit, his face streaked with oil and blood from a gash on his forehead, spoke to him.

"Are you from the *Oriental Monarch*?"

"Yes. We are."

"Thank you very much. It's been frightful on shore. Unbelievable. I'm the British vice consul. Our office was wrecked and the consul was killed, and most of our staff, I guess, but I was lucky. I thought your ship might catch fire, but she seems to be safe."

"We got away from the pier just in time," Perkins told him. "Right now we're anchored with a freighter and we're fouled on her anchor cable. We'll have to do something, but I guess it won't be till morning."

"Do you have survivors aboard?"

"Yes, we do. People who were seeing friends off on the pier came aboard—the ones who weren't killed when the quake hit. I don't know how many people fell through the cracks in the pier. Do you know a family named Bridgeman?"

"Yes. Bridgeman. Yes. A British family. Works here."

"I'm afraid they were lost, but their children are safe. I found them on the pier and brought them aboard."

"Oh. How awful. How awful. A lovely family. Are you sure they're gone?"

"I'm afraid so, unless by some miracle—"

The vice consul bowed his head, shaking it, and fingered the gash on his brow, while Perkins concentrated on bringing the lifeboat alongside the port gangway. Overhead, the late afternoon sky had turned a pale, calm blue, a soft, ironic contrast to the scene of smashed buildings and pillars of smoke. The oil-covered water shone slickly, rainbows of iridescence glinting in the slanting light. He was constantly busy at the tiller avoiding flotsam in the water, afraid to turn the overloaded boat too sharply.

When they came alongside, the refugees were quietly docile as crewmembers directed them aboard. Some needed help; all moved as in a daze.

Stratford was at the gangway, scanning the scene anxiously, aghast at the condition of the refugees. Quickly, he organized stewards to lead the people to the large third-class washrooms to help them in cleaning up. The vice consul came up to him as one of the last to leave.

"Thank you Mr. Stratford."

Stratford peered at him in surprise. "Mr. Wheeler! From the consulate. It is you? Good God, man. Are you all right?"

"I'm alive," Wheeler said. "There are many who are not. All of our staff, I fear. I was standing in the frame of a doorway when the building collapsed, and it protected me. The others were all caught under the ceilings smashing down. I—I—I don't think anyone else survived. It took me some time to get out from under the wreckage, and then I just got down to the water in front of the flames. Most of these people have been standing up to their necks in the water all afternoon to keep away from the fire. The heat was frightful."

"Are there more survivors along the shore?" Stratford asked.

"Yes. Hundreds, I would say. Can you take more aboard?"

"Oh, yes. We'll have to. The captain has already ordered rescue work. We're setting up an emergency hospital, and the passengers have organized to give clothes to these poor wretches. Some of them are almost naked, and in rags."

"I should like to do whatever I can to help," Wheeler said. "I'm afraid I'm the senior surviving official."

"I'll take you up to the bridge," Stratford told him. "You must have some help yourself, and I'm sure the captain will want to work with you."

They started to make their way through the crowded passageways toward the bridge.

"You're lucky you weren't caught in the fire," Wheeler said. "We were sure the ship was going to be caught while we stood there in the water."

"We just got away in time, but now we're fouled with that freighter off our stern," replied Stratford. "We can't move at the moment, but we can't stay here too long."

When they got to the bridge, the captain was directing two more lifeboats to be launched for rescue efforts on shore.

"Captain, this is Mr. Wheeler from the British consulate," Stratford said. "Our lifeboat picked him up at the beach."

"Oh, yes. Wheeler. Good God, man. You look a wreck. What can we do for you? You're injured."

"Just cuts and bruises," Wheeler murmured. "But I'm the only one who got out of the consulate when it collapsed. I'm sure the others were all killed."

"Terrible, terrible," Sam cried. "First we'll have to give you some clothes and see to that cut. Would a drink help you? I have some brandy in my medicine cabinet."

"Yes, it might," Wheeler smiled weakly.

"Chin Ching," Sam called. "Come help this gentleman." The steward came out of the captain's quarters and stood quietly. "First a shot of brandy, and then find him some clothes. I'm afraid mine will be a bit roomy, but one of the officer's things must fit."

"Yes, Captain," Chin Ching bowed his head.

"Thank you, Captain." Wheeler started for the door. "I want to do what I can to help. I'm probably the only one left from the European consulates."

"Were all the others wrecked?" Sam asked, his heart beating faster.

"I'm afraid so. The whole area was in ruins along our street, but I left in a frightful hurry with the flames right behind me."

Wheeler followed Chin Ching inside.

Standing deep in thought, Sam shook himself and turned to Stratford.

"We must have a terrible problem with these refugees," he said. "How are we faring?"

"We're sending them to the third-class washrooms to clean up as best as possible. The doctor is setting up his emergency station at the suites, and we've found two passenger doctors who are helping. We haven't been able to move that Davidoff from the Yokohama Suite. He refused to open up for Holden and me."

"A nasty case. I knew he would be trouble. I guess I had better go talk to him. We'll need that space."

"I'm afraid that's a good idea," Stratford agreed. "I

told him it was captain's orders that he move, but he refused to open."

"Let's go there. I can't leave the bridge for long, but Mr. Davidoff is going to have to cooperate."

Leaving Robertshaw in charge, the two men went to the boat deck passageway and knocked on the Yokohama door. There was no answer.

Sam knocked more firmly.

"Mr. Davidoff. This is Captain Applebye. I must ask you to open up, sir."

There was still no answer.

"Bastard's playing possum," Stratford muttered. "I'll get the steward's master key." He went down the passageway to the steward's station and came back with the key, as Sam knocked several more times with no result.

Stratford worked the key, and they pushed the door in. The room was unlit, and the only light came in through the door to the small verandah deck outside.

"Mr. Davidoff," Sam called.

He started across the room and half tripped over something on the floor.

"What the—" he started. "Good God. Turn on the light."

Davidoff was lying on his back on the carpet, with a large bloodstain spread across his shirtfront and white suit coat. His eyes were open and rolled up into his head, and his mouth was agape in a twisted snarl. Sam leaned down and felt his pulse.

"Gone," he said, looking up. "What the hell?"

"Was it a bullet?"

"I should think so. Do you see a gun anywhere? Could he have done it himself?"

"You'd think somebody would have heard it." Stratford was pale and almost gagging.

They looked around in the carpet, but there was no gun.

"Not with all the roar outside," Sam said matter-of-factly. "But the door was locked. He must have let somebody in. How else?"

"From the verandah?" Stratford asked.

The verandah door was not locked as they tested it.

"Somebody could have climbed up the lifeboat davits and come in through the verandah, I guess." Sam paused, looking around the suite. "Just what we need now! God damn, what a fix." They looked at each other helplessly.

"There's nothing we can do now," Sam said quietly. "There's too much else to be done to be playing detective now. We'll have to get him out of here and put him in the cooler."

"The authorities?" Stratford asked weakly.

"Authorities be blowed," Sam answered. "They're probably all dead on shore, and how can we get in touch anyway? This is just another casualty of the quake for now. I don't like to think of a murderer loose on board, but I'll bet he was only after this one. He was not known for making friends."

"If he'd taken those children in, this might not have happened," Stratford said. "What shall we do?"

"The fewer people that know about this the better," Sam said. "I'll send Chin Ching down with the emergency stretcher from the bridge. Put a sheet over Davidoff and take him down to the icebox, the morgue corner. We've used it before when there is a death aboard, and there'll be more bodies in there before this is over, I'll wager. Chin Ching is completely reliable. He won't talk about it to anyone."

"We'll be noticed."

"Yes, you'll be noticed, but with all this confusion and

casualties all over the place, you'll be noticed as handling a quake casualty, that's all. It's all we can do for now. I'm not going to lose the whole ship over the fate of this gentleman, and then who's to care? It's dicey, I know, but we'll have to decide later on what more we can do. I'll send Chin Ching right down. Oh, yes, and his luggage will have to be stowed. Let's see."

They went into the bedroom. Davidoff's suitcase, opened but unpacked, was on the berth.

"That's easy, then," Sam said. "Just close it up and put it in the locker. Does he have any friends or companions on board?"

"I don't think so. He came aboard alone."

"We'll hope so. No time for people asking questions; but I guess he won't be missed." He started for the door as Stratford began to close the suitcase. "What next, eh? What next, Stratford?" Sam shook his head as he started back to the bridge. Indeed, what next, he thought. A murder aboard would have been an overwhelming problem normally, but now it was just one more blow in the series of unbelievable blows. "No more trouble," flashed through his mind again.

PART

II

MADELAINE WENT into the bathroom and took the paregoric bottle out of the cabinet. She started to unscrew the cap, and then hesitated. She wanted badly to take a spoonful, but the low murmur of the children's voices from the sitting room made her stop. No. She couldn't take the easy way out now. She had to do everything she could for them. Slowly, she put the bottle back on the shelf and closed the door. Turning, she took hold of the towel rack for support and stood for a moment, bowed over, collecting herself. With a deep, shaking sigh, she stood up and went back outside. Peter and Susan were sitting quietly on the settee, their faces drawn and their eyes round and frightened. Susan still sobbed softly and gave small hiccups.

"Are you hungry, children?" she asked.

Peter started to nod no, but Susan spoke in a tight little voice. "I am."

"We have some fruit in this basket. Apples and pears. Would that be nice?"

"Yes, please," both children answered.

"Hannah can make us some tea. We can make our own tea and coffee in these suites, and I think there's some ginger ale in the cooler. We have our own ice box. Isn't that nice?"

They nodded silently. Hannah came out of the other bedroom and began to cut slices of fruit with the paring knife on the tray next to the basket. Madelaine went to the ice box and brought out a bottle of ginger ale and some of the chipped ice that was in a bucket, pouring two glasses. The children took them carefully, both murmuring "Thank you."

"I don't know what will happen to meals with all this awful fuss going on," Madelaine said. "I guess we're lucky to have the fruit. Do you like fruit?" she asked, trying to be light and friendly and avoid silences.

"Oh, yes, thank you," Peter answered.

"Will Mummy and Daddy come for us?" Susan suddenly asked.

"Oh, dear—oh, not right now." Madelaine felt a great pang of shock and sadness. She tried to think of something to say, but Peter spoke first.

"They won't be coming, Susan. They won't be coming."

"Never?"

"Never."

She bit her lip and stared into space.

"Will we live here?" Susan asked. "This is a ship, not a house."

"You'll be here for a while, Susan," Madelaine put in. "Everything is very mixed up because of the earthquake. Do you know what an earthquake is, dear?"

"I don't know. I never heard of one."

"It's when the ground breaks up and tumbles things around. It's a very bad...thing." She finished lamely.

"The earthcake just happened to us when we were looking at the ship and waving," Susan said. "Then we couldn't find Mummy and Daddy." She started to cry again and buried her head against Peter's shoulder.

"I'm afraid she doesn't understand." Peter looked gravely up at Madelaine. "I guess we can't go ashore, can we?"

"No dear. We're out in the harbor now, and all the houses on shore are wrecked or on fire. This is the best place to be."

"We don't have any clothes or money," Peter said.

"Oh, dear," Madelaine cried. "Don't worry about that. You're safe now, and we'll work things out when everything settles down. Soon the doctor is going to have his hospital here, taking care of the people who have been hurt. We'll have to do what we can to help the injured people. Is your arm all right now, Peter?"

"Oh yes, miss. It doesn't bother me now. I can move it, but it is a bit sore."

"Well, be careful of it. Now have your ginger ale and some pieces of apple. We'll all feel better if we eat something. I'm sorry I don't have any cookies."

"This is fine, miss," Peter said. "Thank you very much."

"Thank you," Susan whispered, taking small sips from her glass. "But I want Mummy and Daddy." She suddenly burst into tears again.

There was a knock on the door and Hannah went to open it. Several stewards carrying boxes were in the passageway, and seamen were behind them with the doctor's cabinets on luggage carts.

"Doctor say come here," the first steward announced.

"Oh, yes, come in," Madelaine said. "We are expecting you."

"Some things come here, some to other cabins," the steward hesitated.

"Well, I suppose so. I think all the suites on this corridor are going to be the hospital."

Hannah looked across at the Yokohama Suite. "The door's open over there," she said. "It seems to be open."

Just then Doctor Holden hurried up. "Are you ready for this?" he asked Madelaine anxiously.

"Yes. You warned us. Please do what you have to and tell us if we can help."

"Oh, thank you. Thank you." He looked at the Yokohama

door. "Mr. Davidoff seems to have moved. Well, that's a help."

Holden directed the placing of his equipment in the sitting rooms of the suites. Peter and Susan sat in awed silence watching the activity. Madelaine disappeared into the bedroom, and Hannah bustled about helping the workers. Something would have to be done about the children, Holden thought. He went into the bedroom to talk to Madelaine and found her standing by the porthole staring out, her shoulders shaking.

"Miss Clare—" he said quietly. She continued to stand with her back to him, and he came closer. "Miss Clare, we must do something with the children. I—"

She turned quickly to him and he saw that tears were streaming down her cheeks. With a little cry, she stumbled toward him and he put his arms around her. After a moment, she gained some control and looked up at him.

"I'm sorry," she murmured through sobs. "I'm sorry to be so upset. The poor dears are so confused, and Peter is trying to be so brave. I don't know what to say to them. Susan kept asking when her Mummy and Daddy were coming. I—I just don't know—"

"Yes," he said. "It's terrible, and you've been wonderful to take them in." He hesitated, then asked, "Have you taken any of your, ah, medicine?"

"The paregoric?" She gave a weak smile. "No. I thought it might confuse me, and—but I wanted to," she admitted. "I've got to be strong now." She stepped back with an embarrassed smile. "The children can stay in the bedroom for now. They should be sleepy before too long after all they've been through."

"That's probably the best idea," he said. "You sure you're all right? This is going to be a mess."

"I hope I am. We'll see. How about you? You look tired."

"Nothing unusual, that. I'll be fine."

She put her hand up to his cheek in a gentle gesture, and their eyes held for a moment.

"To work, to work!" he said, turning away, and the thought went through his mind that he didn't know now where the vodka bottle was. He needed it. He needed it, but it would have to wait. If she could be strong, so would he. Some casualties were already in the passageway. He squared his shoulders and stepped out to meet the first one.

Back on the bridge, Sam could not free his mind of the image of Davidoff's bloodstained shirt and gaping mouth as he tried to concentrate on ship's business again. Wheeler and Loomis were there in shirts and pants borrowed from the ship's officers, exchanging the stories of what they had been through. They looked at Sam expectantly.

"Our boats are bringing more refugees," Sam said to them. "We'll be very crowded before long."

"Can the ship handle all that?" Wheeler asked.

"We're fairly well organized. Those who can walk about are to be fed in the second-class dining room, bread-line fashion—just soup and stew and that sort of thing. We've set up an emergency sick bay in the suite area on the boat deck. More room to handle things, and some passenger doctors are going to help our doctor. The stewards have made a lot of tea to help with the burn injuries, and we're using sheets and towels from our linen supply for bandages. We're doing what we can."

"That's remarkable, Captain." Wheeler said. "The whole thing is just beyond belief!"

"Speaking of food, I trust my steward can find us some sandwiches. We must make do with what we can. I'm glad you've been able to clean up a bit, at least."

"Oh, yes. Thank you," Wheeler answered. "I feel I should make a check of the Europeans among the refugees if that is agreeable, Captain. We'll have to try to make some sense out of all the confusion, and we must have a list of survivors prepared."

"Indeed, that's a fine idea and very helpful, if you will see to that," Sam said. "Our staff is so busy trying to organize some sort of order that we haven't done anything like that, yet, I fear."

"Naturally. I'll see what I can do."

"Mr. Loomis, I think I have an assignment for you." Sam turned to the Hong Kong pilot, who had been watching the lifeboats in their trips back and forth from the beach.

"What is that, sir?"

"This freighter astern of us has lost all her officers. She only has deckhands and engineers left, and they will need someone with knowledge when we try to move tomorrow morning. Do you think you could take over?"

"Certainly, sir, if that is needed. Lost all her officers, did she?"

"Yes. Terrible. Very short-handed she is, and we're hung up on her port anchor cable."

"I'll stand by, Captain."

"I'll arrange it soon. I've talked to the bosun, a Scandinavian chap, I believe. We'll work it out when I get a chance. I want to see how our lifeboats are doing."

"There is one terrible problem I heard about just before getting into your lifeboat," Wheeler said. "It seems that the big park about a half-mile inland is full of refugees; only place they could escape the flames. They've been without water for hours. I gather they suffered badly in the heat from the flames."

"Are they locals or Europeans?"

"Mostly Japanese, I believe. I know you couldn't take them all aboard, and they probably want to stay ashore anyhow, but it might help to take them water."

"We'll see," Sam said. "We will if we can. I imagine the

boats have pretty well cleared the shoreline of the people like yourself who were standing in the water. The boats coming back now have very few people in them. I suggest you might work at the sick bay on the boat deck to make your list of survivors, as a start, anyway. Many of them will have to come there for first aid. Then you can check in the other areas. There's a room there you can use. We've, ah...moved the passenger out."

Evening twilight had almost faded by now, and the small fires still burning in some shore areas stood out more vividly. Here and there a searchlight beam stabbed through the gloom, but there were no other lights visible in the ruined city. Around the harbor some of the ships showed lights, and a few wrecked boats still had small fires burning. As the darkness gathered, the multi-tiered lights of the *Monarch* cast long reflections across the oily sheen of the harbor. The far horizon inland was aglow with the loom of distant fires.

Sam had checked every lifeboat load coming from shore with the binoculars, hoping against hope that he would see Mikaela. His anxiety for her was becoming an obsession. It was almost too much to realize that at about this time the evening before they had been making love. The sense of that, the memory of it, made him shiver. Her beauty, her warmth, the feel of her in his arms, the touch of her skin, of her soft hair against his cheek came back to him in a rush of sensation, overwhelming him in desperation. If only he could go ashore and search for her, find out something. The urge to do this was overpowering, but he knew it was impossible. Every minute of his training from the first day he went to sea made him know that he could not leave the ship. "God damn duty," Mikaela had said, and he cursed at the irony of it. God damn duty anyway.

Chin Ching materialized out of the darkness of the

officers' deck aft of the bridge, carrying a tray with sandwiches and tea. He silently passed it to the three men.

"Ah, Chin Ching. Good man. Eat while we can," Sam said to the others as they all took sandwiches and started to eat quickly.

The presence of the silent Chinaman suddenly gave Sam in idea, and he excused himself from the others and beckoned Chin Ching into his quarters.

"Thank you, Chin Ching. This is a very difficult time."

"Yes, Captain. Difficult."

"Aah," Sam started, not knowing how to begin. "Chin Ching. I would like to ask a great favor of you."

"Anything, Captain."

"I simply cannot leave the ship now. I'm sure you realize that."

"Oh, yes."

"And I am very worried about the person I was with last night. I was hoping she might come as a refugee, but I have not seen her. I don't know if she is injured or dead, and I am very worried."

"Maybe I find her." Chin Ching looked up, and their eyes met. "I know her house."

"It might be very dangerous. I cannot order you to go."

"I go. Lifeboats going ashore still?"

"Yes, they are, and I'm going to order Mr. Perkins to organize a party to take water to the people in the park. I understand they are desperate. You can go with that crew and make a search while they are taking the water to the people. She might have been at the Swedish consulate, but I think she would have gone home to lunch by the time the quake hit. I would go there first."

"Yes, Captain."

"Her name is Mikaela Swenson."

Sam phoned the gangway and asked the purser on duty to send Perkins to the bridge when his boat came alongside.

Back on the bridge wing, he spoke to Loomis. "Mr. Loomis, perhaps it might help if you were to go aboard the *Cape Fear* now. You can familiarize yourself with the setup tonight, because tomorrow we will have to do something about moving. I'm very uneasy with the situation as we are, but at least we're in a good spot for rescue operations now."

"I'm ready, Captain," Loomis answered.

"We'll see about transferring you. I think the ships are close enough for you to do it."

Just then, Perkins arrived on the bridge, his boyishly handsome face streaked with oil and sweat, his uniform a soggy, oily mess. "You sent for me, Captain?"

"Yes, Mr. Perkins. Good God, man, you look a wreck."

"I'm all right, Captain. It's pretty messy in the boat with all those people covered in oil and all soaking wet. They're a sad sight."

"Yes, indeed. Well, I think you had better change into some work clothes, because I have another job for you. We want to send some breakers of water to refugees in the park inland. I've been told that they're in desperate need. Can you find a spot to land?"

"There's the remains of a small boat pier we can get alongside. I took the first group of people right out of the water, because they were already in it and coming out to us as soon as we got here. But we've used the pier on the last couple of trips. People have been waiting there for us."

"Do you have enough men to handle the water breakers? You'll need luggage carts to take them up to the park, I think."

"Yes sir. We'll manage. My boat crew has been superb."

"One more thing," the captain went on. "Chin Ching is going to go ashore on a special mission for me. I want you to take him with you and then arrange for meeting him to come back. I don't want him left there."

"Oh, no sir. Of course." Perkins left to change his clothes and Chin Ching appeared silently at Sam's side.

"It's all set, Chin Ching," Sam told him. "Mr. Perkins is changing to work clothes and then he will be taking water ashore with a work crew. You can go with him, and you should make definite arrangements for coming back. You must take a torch with you. There's no light on shore." He hesitated, then went on. "I do appreciate this—and do be careful. I'm asking a lot of you."

"Yes, Captain; I understand. Captain, I make eyewash for you. Is on sink in head. It make eyes better, I hope."

"Thank you, thank you, Chin Ching. That's very thoughtful. I do need it."

Perkins came back in khaki work uniform, and Chin Ching followed him off the bridge. It was a thin, desperate hope that Sam sent with them, but there was no more he could do now. He sighed deeply and suddenly realized how tired he was. Perhaps he could use the eye solution before he took Loomis back to the *Cape Fear*. His eyes had been burning and itching painfully. He remembered that once before Chin Ching had made him a boric solution ("bolic", he chuckled), and it had been a help. It was going to be a long night.

"I'll be right with you, Mr. Loomis," he said. "Just give me a minute and then we'll see about the *Cape Fear*."

He went into his quarters, picked up the glass of eyewash, and stretched out on his bunk, applying it carefully with cotton. Suddenly, he felt weak and overwhelmed, as the soothing liquid took some of the sting out of his eyes. Things were quiet now, but there was still the tremendous problem in getting the ship, crippled as she was, out into open water, and the thought of the hundreds of refugees seemed appalling. Then there was Davidoff's murder, and his body. Never, in all his years at sea, had he faced so many problems. He groaned and tried to clear his head, but the whirling kaleidoscope of all the challenges that faced him stayed with him. And through it all, the terrible uncertainty about what might have happened to Mikaela preyed on him. If only he could go to sleep and wipe out the whole scene; if only he and Mikaela were off together in some quiet hideaway and the world was far, far away.

"God damn duty," he muttered. He struggled off the bed to a sitting position, shook himself, and went back out to the bridge wing. Loomis was there, looking off across the harbor at the odd jumble of ships' lights, dying fires on shore, and the distant glow on the horizon in the direction of Tokyo.

"I've never seen anything like this," he said quietly as Sam came to his side. "Never, in all my days. It must be one of the world's worst."

"Yes, Mr. Loomis. I agree," Sam said. "And we'll be part of it if we can't get the vessel out of here. All's quiet now, but I don't feel safe at all."

"Yes, there will be more fires, and even more shocks."

"Are you sure you want to take over on the freighter?" Sam asked. "I have no idea what the situation is except for the fact her officers are all gone, but I don't see how we can maneuver out of here without the two ships working together."

"I know the ship, Captain," Loomis said. "I've had her in Hong Kong once or twice. Scandinavian, I believe; a single screw vessel. I think we can work it. Have you figured out your own condition?"

"We only have the starboard screw," Sam answered, "and I'm almost afraid to use that with all the wreckage under the stern. I know our port screw is fouled—on the freighter's anchor cable, I think. I'd hate to lose both screws. We'd be helpless then, even more than we are now." He paused. "You're not injured? You can handle this?"

"Scratches and bruises. Nothing like most of the poor bastards I've seen coming aboard. I was lucky on the pier."

"Let's go back there and see if we can get you aboard," Sam said. They started off the bridge and took the starboard promenade deck. It was quiet now, compared to the frantic scene in the afternoon when the flames were mounting outside and the hoses were playing. A few people were lying in deck chairs, and every once in a while a passenger would come out from one of the saloons and look anxiously across the rail at the dark shore, dimly outlined in the loom of fires.

"Passengers getting something more than they booked this time," Loomis grunted.

"So far they have been most helpful—magnificent, in fact," Sam answered. "They've been helping take care of the injured, loaning out their clothes, taking refugees into their cabins, and standing in line for their meals. Nobody's complaining. I've never had a situation like this."

"Nobody has, I'd dare say."

"I thought the typhoon in your harbor was a bad one, but that was nothing compared to this."

They arrived at the fantail, and Sam hailed a man standing watch on the *Cape Fear*'s deck.

"Is Mr. Christiansen here?" he called.

The man waved in acknowledgement and went off, coming back soon with the bosun.

"Captain Applebye here again, Mr. Christiansen. I have Mr. Loomis with me. He's the Hong Kong pilot and he knows your vessel."

"Yes, Captain. Ve need help."

"He and I will work out the method for getting out of here in the morning. Right now, we have many boats picking up refugees from the shore, and we must stay here. It seems as though we are safe for now, but I'm most anxious to clear out in the morning."

"Aye, sir. That is good. I get gangplank here in a minute." He went off down the deck.

"We'll have to confer in the morning, Loomis. It looks as though you will have to tow us out to the turning basin, because I can't run to starboard with my port screw fouled. It'll be tricky."

"I think we can work it sir. I'll stand by and be ready in the morning."

Christiansen and a deckhand came back with a plank and pushed it across through the *Monarch*'s railing. Loomis, shaking hands with Sam, moved across it carefully and waved back.

"In the morning," Sam called, and headed back to the bridge.

Perkins was at the gangway organizing his crew and directing them in putting the breakers of water and luggage carts into the lifeboat. Chin Ching stood quietly by. The area was now clear of refugees, and there had only been a few small boats coming alongside with more in the last hour. One of the other lifeboats was on a trip ashore, but the frantic scene had quieted.

A tall man Perkins recognized as Mr. Simms from the fuel company, the American who had helped people on the pier, was talking to one of the assistant pursers at the end of the gangway. He turned to Perkins. "Taking water ashore?" he asked.

"That's right. Yes sir."

"Do you need help? I know the lay of the land pretty well. I've been living here. Maybe I can help you find your way."

"That would be very kind. But it might be dangerous."

"Couldn't be any more dangerous than this noon on the pier," Simms said. "I'd like to help."

"Well, fine. We're all set, I think. Water's aboard; carts for carrying it, dippers, torches. I think we're ready to go."

Simms and Chin Ching followed Perkins down to the

boat, and they cast off and started for the shore. One of the seaman in the bow picked out pieces of wreckage with a hand searchlight and Perkins stood at the tiller, threading his way through. Tired as he was, he felt a sudden burst of exhilaration, of confidence, that he had been given the responsibility. It was frightening, but it was a challenge.

Chin Ching was sitting next to Simms, separated from the working party of seamen.

"Are you with the water party?" Simms asked him. "You're the captain's steward, aren't you? I think I've seen you when I've been up at his quarters."

"Yes sir. I do special job for captain."

"Good God, I hope you're careful. It will be rough on shore."

"I know. I look for one person."

"Where? In this mess?"

"Maybe find, maybe not."

"Where are you looking?"

"House on Bund; maybe Swedish consulate."

"Swedish consulate? Ah, yes. I think I know. Yes. I have seen the captain with someone."

Chin Ching said no more, and they fell silent until the boat slowed, making an odd gurgling sound in its passage through the oil-heavy water, and eased alongside the remains of a small boat pier. It was half in the water, but there was enough of it left to provide a passage to the beach. The work crew heaved the water breakers onto the pier one by one and manhandled them to the shore, along with the luggage carriers. When everything was assembled, they started across the beach to the boulevard that headed uphill and inland. Chin Ching, who had arranged timing with Perkins on meeting for the return trip, moved off quietly into the darkness. The work party, with Simms and Perkins in the lead, started up the hill, leaving one man, armed with a revolver, to stay with the boat. There was a pervading, acrid stench in the air, almost suffocating in its bitterness.

Perkins coughed and covered his mouth. "Whew, what a stink," he muttered.

"Even worse than I thought it would be," Simms said.

Shining their lights ahead of them, they had to make frequent detours and diversions around wide holes in the street and ridges where the pavement had heaved up. There were bodies lying on the ground, and here and there an automobile was on its side or turned over. Off in the darkness on either side of the street occasional faint cries could be heard. Every once in a while, a dog skittered away in panic, or a human figure could be seen sidling along. When they had gone a few hundred yards, a body of men with lanterns and long bamboo sticks with knives lashed at the end came charging out of the darkness toward them and blocked their way with crossed sticks, shouting in Japanese.

Perkins and his Chinese seamen stopped in confusion, but Simms stepped forward and talked to them in Japanese. After some excited shouting, they calmed down and exchanged words with Simms. Finally, they stepped aside and pointed up the hill with the makeshift spears.

"They say they are a police patrol," Simms explained, "There are a great many survivors still in the park, and the water should be a big help. They say that the jails have broken open and gangs of prisoners are out looting. When they saw your Chinamen, at first they thought that's what they might be. The prisoners are mostly Koreans. There's no love lost between Koreans and Japanese, and it sounds like a dangerous situation. They told us to be careful."

"They wouldn't get much from us but water," Perkins said. "I guess we should have been armed." He spoke to the leader of the work gang. "Some of you have knives, I hope. Keep them ready."

They started on their difficult way again, and, as they

drew out of the foreign quarter, where the buildings had all been brick and concrete and were in piles of rubble, they came to an area where wooden houses had stood. These were completely burned out, with bitter smoke still curling up from a few of the ruins. Up ahead, they began to hear a low, disturbed murmuring that grew louder until they recognized that it was the sound from a huge mob of people. They were at the park, an open space of trees and shrubs, and it could gradually be seen that it was a solid mass of people, mostly standing still, with an occasional eddy of motion, in darkness relieved here and there by a small flicker of light from a flashlight and the distant loom of fires on the northern horizon that cast a dim, eerie glow.

"My God, how do we handle this?" Perkins asked Simms in a low voice. "We'll get mobbed if they know what we have."

"I don't know. These would be very frightened people, but they are disciplined. I've dealt with them a lot, working here. I'll find someone to talk to, either in English or my pretty crude Japanese."

Perkins and his crew huddled together in silence as the tall figure of Simms, standing high above the rest of the people, moved into the edge of the crowd. Thank God he came, Perkins thought. I wouldn't know how to handle this. Each movement of someone at the outer rim of the mob made him start in alarm, each little bit of motion was an imagined threat. He noticed that his men, clustered close behind him, had drawn their knives and held them at the ready. He wouldn't know a Korean from a Japanese, Chinaman, or Filipino in broad daylight, much less in this weird gloom. The sweat rolled down inside his shirt and his throat grew dry while he waited. For a while he lost sight of Simms' tall figure, but then he could be seen coming back, and Perkins felt a flood of relief.

"I've found a policeman," Simms said. "He's going to

pass the word, and people will queue up for a dipper of water each. I don't think there'll be a riot. They're all too scared. He's going to tell women with children to come first. Each one is to get one dipper full."

The ship's crew put the breakers on the ground and opened the tops. Soon a silent line started forming in the gloom in front of them, directed by Simms and the policeman. One by one they came forward, with many of the children crying softly. The crew ladled the dippers and handed them out. Some were gulped in an instant, while others were taken in small sips, with the sobs of the children slowly subsiding.

Suddenly there was an eruption of shouting and shoving back in the line and a single figure of a man broke from it and started running toward them. The Japanese policeman who had been standing by the water moved quickly to meet him, shouting orders. Instead of stopping, the man came on in a frenzy, starting to grapple with the policeman. Avoiding wrestling with him, the policeman took one step backward, pulled out a knife, and plunged it into the man's chest. There was a gargled cry, a last frantic clutching of arms in empty air, and the man fell to the ground. The policeman, using his boots, then kicked and rolled the body to one side, came calmly back to the line, and motioned the next woman forward.

Perkins had hardly been aware of what was happening before it was over, and he stared dumbly at the body, half in shock.

"There won't be any more trouble," Simms murmured.

The ladling went on in orderly fashion as the crowd slowly inched forward. Perkins found himself aware that he too was extremely thirsty. He couldn't remember when he had last had anything to eat or drink, or had been to the bathroom. He grunted in irony and continued to watch the crowd.

Finally all the water was gone. They collected the empty

casks, loaded them on the carriers, and started the tortuous way back down to the waterfront, promising the policeman that the ship would send more water later. While they threaded their way through the potholes and debris of the boulevard, Perkins wondered whether Chin Ching would be back at the lifeboat as arranged. He didn't want to wait around at the shoreline if Chin Ching wasn't there, but he did have orders from the captain. He kept a wary eye on the surrounding darkness, visualizing Korean prisoners charging at them, but the way was deserted until they finally reached the shore. Chin Ching was not there, and the seaman who had been guarding the boat had not seen him.

When Chin Ching faded into the darkness as the work crew started up the boulevard to the park, his way was almost blocked by the piles of rubble strewn across the wide surface of the Bund. He picked his way carefully, using his flashlight now and then, and moving as silently as he could. It was very difficult to keep his bearings as to how far he had gone along the Bund, so confusing were the heaps of stones, the breaks in the pavement, and the odd gaps in the skyline, where tall buildings had once been, showing the glow of northern fires in the direction of Tokyo. A dog scuttled away as he paused in front of one pile of stones, startling him for a moment. From the buildings came an overpowering miasma of burning and destruction, and an occasional wisp of smoke, though there were no more open fires.

He was trying to locate the side street at the corner where Mikaela's building had been. Some time ago, when the captain had given him her address, as he went ashore to join her, Chin Ching had followed to make sure he knew where the building was, but he had not been there otherwise.

From the remains of a building next to him he heard low guttural rumblings and smashing noises. He turned out his light and stood silently behind a pile of stones. Working in a dim lantern light, three men were pulling planks and stones away from what had been the display room of a store for Western clothes. Chin Ching saw that they were gathering clothing in their arms and loading it onto a wheelbarrow. From what he could hear of their talk to each other in low voices, he knew it was not Japanese, and he figured it must be Korean, a language he did not know. Their actions seem furtive and hasty, and he realized they had to be looters. He had been thinking of asking them what the location was, but he changed his mind and shrunk back lower as they charged out of the store and came by him. Their eyes shone wildly in the slants of dim light, and there was a strong smell of stale sweat when they went by. He ducked lower and held his breath. If looters were around, his job would be more dangerous than ever.

When they had gone, he moved cautiously on, using the light as little as possible. Whenever there were nearby noises of people moving, his heart came into his mouth. He did not want to run into Korean looters, and, also, police might be about. Since he could not talk to them, he would be in trouble with them too. They would probably think he was a looter. Making his way along, he put out his hand to feel his way around an obstruction and recoiled quickly, with a low gasp. It was a big piece of timber that was still hot from a fire, and a few small sparks fell away from where his hand had touched. Sometimes his foot slipped into a hole, making him stagger, but he was moving so slowly and cautiously that he didn't fall.

The clothing store had given him a reference, and he remembered now that it was another block to the corner where the Swedish woman's building was. When he finally made it that far, picking his way around obstacle after obstacle and skirting potholes, some with water in them, he decided that the pile of stones on the east side must be what was left of the building. He could see the area, barely defined with all the rubble on it, that must have been the side street. No one was about, and he moved carefully toward the wreckage, feeling his way, and shining the flashlight in short bursts.

It looked hopeless. In the darkness, there was no pattern to the piles of stones and broken timbers to tell where the entrance might have been, and he had no idea of what to do next. It seemed impossible that anyone could have lived in the collapse of this building, and he was just wondering whether he should try to find the Swedish consulate, when he heard a low cry from somewhere in the wreckage.

"Yes," he called. "Yes. Anyone there?"

Another moan, a bit louder came back. Moving toward it, he called out again, and got another answer, a faint "Here. Here." It was a woman's voice.

At first, the piles of stones seemed solid, and he could see no way to get through them toward the cry, but, using the light, he worked his way carefully forward, squeezing through some close openings. As he came around one pile and put his foot down, it slid sideways off something soft. He gasped and shone the light down, and the body of a man was face down on the ground, a heavy timber across his back, his head twisted at an impossible angle. A pool of blood lay under him. Chin Ching choked back a gasp and stepped carefully around into a more open space.

The low moans were closer as he moved forward, and he called out again. "Yes. Yes."

He was answered by more soft cries of "Here, here," which grew louder while he moved. Then his light hit on something white. It looked like a woman's thigh sticking out from under a timber. When he got to it and shone the light on the other side, there was a woman's pale face, streaked in dust, and her eyes glittered in the light.

"Please help me," she said in a faint voice. "I can't move."

"Yes. I help," Chin Ching said. "You Miss Swenson?"

"Yes. Yes I am," she answered, her voice breaking.

"I Captain Applebye steward. He send me for you."

"Oh, thank God, thank God," she cried. "It's been so long. I can't move this piece of wood."

"You hurt bad?" he asked.

"I don't know. Everything hurts, but I don't know."

"Let me see if I can move wood. It look very heavy."

He shone the light around the area and saw that the timber was under a heavy section of stone wall at one end and covered with a rubble of stone and wood at the other. He studied the piles of stone and the wall and didn't see how he could possibly move them by himself. If he did, he might make the timber crush down on her more heavily. He tugged at the section of wall and could not move it at all. At the other end, he thought that two people might be able to move the weight off the timber, but he was sure that he could not.

"So bad," he murmured to her. "So heavy. I go get help from ship's crew. They just down by beach."

"Oh," she cried, "don't leave. Don't leave. I'm so afraid." Her left arm was free, and she held it up in a pathetic appeal.

"No can do myself. No can do. I get help quick. Please no afraid. I come right back with help." He gave her hand a squeeze. "I come back quick."

"Oh please, yes. Come quickly."

"Soon. Soon," he said as he wormed his way back out through the wreckage, trying to recognize some way that he could help find the spot again. Finally out on the street, he moved as quickly as possible, knocking his shins on rocks and twice falling into potholes, headed for the lifeboat. He could just see it when he was suddenly surrounded by a group of men who jumped out from behind a section of wall. They grabbed him roughly, held a light into his eyes, and a man with a long bamboo pole with a knife on it held it against his throat, just about to slice it. They were yelling in Japanese.

"No. No. Friend! Friend!" he cried first in Chinese, then in English. They were not the looters he had seen, and he thought they might be militia looking for looters.

"Me from ship. *Monarch* ship." He gestured desperately to the lifeboat, and out to the harbor, where the *Monarch*'s lights tiered brightly into the night. "Ship. Ship. *Monarch* ship," he repeated. He could see up ahead the flashlights of the work crew just arriving back at the lifeboat, and he pointed wildly at it and yelled. The knife pressed against his throat, but the man with the light hesitated and turned to look in the direction of the lifeboat.

"Ask them. Ask them." Chin Ching pointed. "From ship too."

Pushing him roughly along, the group headed for the lifeboat and one of them threw Chin Ching to the ground as they got there. Simms and Perkins heard the noise and turned to look.

"My God! Chin Ching. They've got Chin Ching," Perkins cried.

Simms ran over quickly. It was the same police group that had stopped them on the way up, and he spoke to the leader in Japanese, identifying Chin Ching.

The police officer said there was much looting, but Simms explained the situation, and the police muttered and moved away.

"What's happened, Chin Ching?" Perkins asked.

Chin Ching stood up, rubbing his throat. "They think I Korean looter," he said. "Lucky you here. They kill me maybe." He shook his head. "Swedish woman need help," he went on. "She alive but stuck in wreckage. I can't move, so I come for help. You come quick? You help? We need many men." He pointed down the Bund.

"Come on," Perkins said, gesturing to two of the seamen to bring a stretcher from the boat, and with Simms with them the group headed off, following Chin Ching. His light guided them through the rubble, but they stumbled and cursed as they bumped into stones and timbers, moving as quickly as they could.

"Is she badly hurt?" Perkins asked Chin Ching.

"Maybe. Maybe. Stuck under big timber. Cannot move it myself. She talk to me. She very scared."

With their extra flashlights they found the way more quickly, and Chin Ching pointed the way to the wrecked house when they got to the corner.

"Who is this woman?" Perkins asked.

Before Chin Ching could answer, Simms said, "She is Mrs. Swenson from the Swedish consulate. I believe the captain has been seeing her when the ship's in port."

"Oh," was all Perkins answered.

They moved cautiously into the wrecked jumble of the hour, and Perkins called out, "Mrs. Swenson, Mrs. Swenson."

A faint cry answered from farther inside, and Chin Ching led them along, pointing his light down at the man's body without comment as they all stepped carefully across it.

"Can't help that bugger," Simms muttered.

"I bring help," Chin Ching said as they reached Mikaela.

"Oh, thank you, thank you," came her faint reply.

"Let's be careful," Simms said, looking over the situation. He leaned over, looking down at Mikaela. "Here we are. We'll get you out now. Are you in great pain?"

"I hurt. I hurt all over," she said. "I can't tell what's happened to me, but the weight of this is terrible."

"We're going to be very careful about moving things.

We don't want to make anything shift the wrong way. But we'll have you out of here soon."

"Please. Yes, please. It's been so long and so dark. Is it night now? I can't tell."

"Yes, it is. Quite late. You've had a rough one, and you're very brave."

"I—I don't feel brave," her voice quavered.

Perkins, Simms, and Chin Ching shone their lights over the timber, examining what was holding it in place. The big section of wall at one end looked too heavy and solid to move, and it was blocked by other wreckage. At the other end there were loose stones and smaller sections of wall, and the crew started to move them carefully.

"Don't take supports from underneath," Simms said. "Clear the top of it."

Perkins directed the men, and they all pitched in until they had the end of the timber in the clear.

"Maybe we can pry it up," Perkins said, looking for a strong piece of wood.

"If we lift it a little bit and put more stones under it, we should be able to get her clear. Step by step," Simms said. As he spoke, Mikaela gave a weak scream, and a rat skittered across her leg and out of range of the lights.

"My God," Perkins cried. "Have they been around?"

"Some, yes," she said. "I've been sweeping at them with this one free hand I have. It's so frightening." She sobbed softly.

The second time the whole crew lifted the end of the timber and put a broken piece of concrete under it, Mikaela gave a gasp. "I can move, I think. I can move." She stirred slightly, and her other arm moved across her chest slowly.

"Easy, now. Easy. Any broken bones, do you think?" Simms bent over her. "Don't move too quickly."

"It's my leg that hurts the most," she answered. "My right one."

The stretcher was placed next to her carefully, and inch by inch, taking her by the shoulders and knees, Simms and Perkins moved her sideways until her body was out from under the timber. Her dress was torn and covered with dirt and blood, and her right ankle was oddly bent. When they lifted her as carefully as possible to put her on the stretcher, she gave one sharp cry of pain, then bit her lip and her eyes filled with tears. She reached out and Chin Ching, standing closest, took her hand and let her squeeze his hard.

"Is good now, Miss," he said softly. "We take you to ship and doctor will help you."

"Is the ship all right?" she asked.

"Plenty trouble, but safe so far. She in harbor near pier."

"I'm so glad. It's been so terrible here. Some people were screaming for a while, and then it was quiet. Then I smelled smoke but no fire came here."

"Many fires all over city. City all wrecked."

"Were you in your flat?" Perkins asked her.

"No. I would be dead if I had been, I'm sure. I was just coming in the lobby door from the street when everything started to fall. I just remember being knocked down, with everything crashing, and then I guess I was unconscious for a while. I lost all idea of time, but I was sure I was going to die. I didn't see how anyone could find me. And the rats—" her voice trailed off in sobs.

"Well, you're safe now," Perkins told her.

Moving slowly, trying to keep from jolting the stretcher, the boat crew maneuvered through the wreckage, sometimes having to move stones or a section of wall to make room for the stretcher's passage. Finally they reached the comparatively open area of the Bund, but they still had to pick a way step by step around the piles of rubble and the potholes. Once or twice one of the men stumbled, bringing an involuntary groan from Mikaela. It was slow, difficult work.

While they moved along, Perkins spoke softly to Simms. "I can't thank you enough, sir. We couldn't have handled all this without you."

"Glad to do it. Glad I could."

"How about yourself? Do you have a house?"

"No. A flat near here, just down the Bund a ways. I looked over there earlier. The building was just a pile of bricks."

"Well. You can base on the ship. We're setting up to take care of a lot of people."

"I know, but I have an idea I should stay and try to find out what happened to my things. Luckily I don't have any family to worry about—and come to think of it, no job either. This has been some day. I think I'd better stay ashore, though."

"If you think so." Perkins fell silent.

They were just approaching the boat landing when, out of the darkness from behind what was left of the wall of a house, bodies rushed at them and they were under a murderous attack.

"Koreans," Chin Ching gasped.

In the first rush, the stretcher was jostled roughly. Mikaela screamed, and the bearers put it down quickly, drawing their knives. Simms, Perkins, and Chin Ching recovered from the first attack, which had knocked Perkins to the ground, and, standing close together in front of the stretcher, began to strike back. The attackers were using sticks as clubs, and one had a knife. The smell of their sweat was overpowering. The crewmembers came forward, swinging their knives, and the others started striking back as best they could in the darkness.

"Ho! *Monarch* boat," Perkins bellowed. "*Monarch* boat here. Help! Help!"

The attack was being fiercely pressed, but they couldn't retreat and leave the stretcher unprotected.

"Buggers want our money, the lady's rings," Simms grunted, swinging away at the nearest one. The man's club caught him across the forearm, and he howled in pain and anger, striking back by moving in closely before the man could swing again. There was a piercing scream from another of the attackers as one of the crewmen made contact with his knife, and Perkins, flailing away, continued to yell at the top of his lungs. At last the guard from the boat came running toward them, firing a shot into the air. When they heard the shot the looters quickly dropped back, and Perkins picked up a flashlight from under his feet and shone it at the attackers. The man from the boat leveled the revolver and fired one shot at the group. One man screamed and fell to the ground. The others turned and fled into the darkness.

"Your friends from before, Chin Ching?" Perkins gasped. "What else can happen?"

Catching his breath and peering into the darkness, Perkins muttered to Simms, "All clear, I guess. Thank God for the armed guard. Well done," he said to the seaman. "Let's get out of here."

"Good idea," said Simms, "and I think I'll come with you. The hell with this place."

"Are you all right, Mrs. Swenson?" Perkins bent over her. "Sorry for the bumping around."

"I guess so." She tried a weak smile.

Out of the night, a boat could be heard approaching, and First Mate Barclay brought it alongside astern of Perkins' boat.

"We've got another water detail," Barclay announced. "What's the drill?"

Perkins told him what they had done and how to handle it. As they were talking, a man in a torn, smeared business suit staggered toward them. "*Oriental Monarch, Oriental Monarch*!" came a cry.

"My God, it's Graham," Barclay said. "I thought everyone from the office had been killed."

Breathless and disheveled, Graham came up to them and had to be held from falling.

"Thank God, thank God," he cried. "I've been trapped in the wreckage until just now. The whole building is wrecked. I'm the only one left. The ship's all right? She's still here, I see."

"Yes. She has some damage, and one screw fouled," Perkins said. "We're lashed to a freighter now, and there are hundreds of refugees aboard. We're running water parties to the people up in the park. Thousands of them there homeless."

"I thought I heard shooting just now when I was coming down the hill."

"We were attacked by looters, but our guard has a gun. That got rid of them."

"Looters? The whole city must be wrecked. I smelled fires all the time I was trapped," Graham said. "This is unbelievable, unbelievable."

As he spoke, the ground under them began to shake and jolt, and there was a dull, rumbling sound.

"Oh no!" Perkins yelled. "No more, no more!"

"Aftershocks. I've been feeling them all day," Graham said.

"If I had any idea of staying, that does it," Simms muttered, stepping into the boat. The shock only lasted seconds and the work crew quickly but carefully loaded the stretcher into the boat. Perkins stepped to the tiller, started the engine, and they shoved off as Barclay's party started up the hill to the park.

Graham looked down at the stretcher. "Mikaela Swenson!"

"Hello, George," she said weakly. "You made it too."

"God. I guess very few did. You're injured?"

"My leg, I think. I was trapped under a big piece of

wood until the man from the ship found me. I thought I would die there for so long a time." She gave an involuntary sob.

He took her hand and squeezed it. "I guess you can say we're the lucky ones, and lucky that the ship's still here. I didn't see how she could come through it. Captain Applebye must have done a wonderful job."

"He took in all the people on the pier who were seeing the ship off, including me," Simms said. "The crew fought the fire for quite a while, and the ship was trapped by the freighter astern of her. I thought she was a goner for sure."

"Martin Simms!" Graham said, shaking his hand. "I didn't recognize you in this light."

"I'm not at my best," Simms grunted. "Just glad to be alive."

"But the ship didn't catch fire?"

"When the flames got too much, Applebye just smashed his way out of there, taking the freighter with him. Only thing he could do, and it took guts. One screw's fouled and the ships are stuck together a bit off the pier. The fire's out now, but it would have taken the ship in another couple of minutes. I'm sure of that."

"Well, he's our top captain, you know," Graham said. "He's due to get our new ship in another couple of months."

"If he gets out of this one," Simms muttered.

"Sounds like he's done a fine job so far."

"You can say that again," Simms agreed, "They don't come any better as seamen than Applebye. I thought sure the ship was lost."

Graham bent down to Mikaela, who had been listening. "I thought you might have been at the ship with the Swedish passengers you had boarding."

"I gave them their documents at the consulate. They didn't need any more help, so I went home to lunch. I would have been killed at the consulate, I'm sure, and I would have been killed if I'd gotten home five minutes sooner. I was just in the entrance when the building fell down."

Graham shook his head. "Amazing, isn't it, how a few feet or a couple of minutes can make such a difference. I was in a doorway, too, when the thing hit, so I wasn't under the ceiling when it fell. That's... that's what got everybody else in the office..." His voice trailed off.

The boat was slowing down for the gangway. From her position lying down, Mikaela had the impression that the ship towered far into the night, with its many tiers of lights. It looked so solid and permanent, it was hard for her to grasp that such an immense thing could have been in peril. Would she see Sam, she wondered? He would be so busy, and there would be so many people all about. She longed to see him, but she couldn't imagine how it would be. At least he had sent his man to look for her, and the thought of that was a good one. Chin Ching was looking down at her, and she gave him a warm smile.

"I haven't had a chance to thank you in all the excitement," she said. "You were so good, so wonderful to come for me and find me. I don't know how you did it."

Chin Ching smiled back and bowed his head. "So happy to do," he said softly. "Captain will be so happy you come. We fix you up, get clean, and doctor will help you. You hurt bad now?"

"Yes, it hurts, but I can stand it much better now than when I was all alone in the dark. Thank you again. I don't know your name, and you saved my life."

"Chin Ching my name."

"Oh yes. The captain has mentioned you. So thank you, Chin Ching, thank you."

The boat came alongside under the glare of the gangway light. The work crew handled the stretcher carefully, keeping it level, and Perkins went to the gangway watch.

"We've got more injured people here," he said. "Can

you see that they get to the doctor's station? They both need attention. The man can walk, but the woman is on a stretcher. We've got to make another trip ashore with water when we get these breakers filled."

Chin Ching came off alongside the stretcher, watching the handling carefully. Simms slipped by them and disappeared down the passageway. As the stretcher carriers started toward the elevator, Chin Ching leaned over. "I tell Captain you here," he said softly to Mikaela.

In the Yokohama Suite, Vice Consul Wheeler, in clean shirt and pants, his cuts bandaged and his forehead covered with bruises, was getting organized in the bedroom off the sitting room. He had found a pen and writing paper on the desk, and was ready to start finding out the names and nationalities of European survivors.

Robertshaw came in, looked around the suite, and spoke to Wheeler from the door. "Mr. Wheeler. I'm Staff Captain Robertshaw. I believe we have met at the consulate. Captain Applebye asked me to do what I can to help you."

"Ah. Yes indeed." Wheeler stood up and they shook hands. "That's very kind. I am just beginning to organize, and I hardly know where to start. This is such a frightful thing. I can't believe it. It's a miracle the ship is safe, at least."

"Yes, it is, but I'm very worried. We should have been away from here by now. The ship is being endangered by staying here and doing all this rescue work."

"Oh, but it is so valuable. So important. The poor people have nowhere else to go."

"I believe there are relief agencies ashore."

"There couldn't be anything organized yet. The entire city is in ruins. What didn't fall down burned down, and I'm sure the authorities have been hit just as badly as anyone else. There are probably no hospitals or first-aid squads able

BILL ROBINSON

to operate, and everything is disorganized. The ship being here is a godsend."

"Well. I hope nothing happens. I think it's a needless risk."

"We'll have to see. I'm sure that there are many people who thank God that the risk has been taken."

"Perhaps."

"Can you help me on where to start? There must be refugees from shore all over the ship. By the way, I understand this was Mr. Davidoff's cabin. His suitcase seems to be here, but he must have been moved."

"Yes. We have commandeered all this area for emergency medical work. I'm not sure where he has been moved. Perhaps that was an extra suitcase."

"He's a difficult man. I wouldn't want to run afoul of him. I'm surprised he cooperated at all."

"I believe the captain persuaded him to move," Robertshaw said. "And to start with on your record keeping, there are two children being cared for across the way by Miss Madelaine Clare, the movie actress. I believe their parents were killed on the pier when the quake hit."

"Oh, my. Do you know their name? Is it Bridgeman by any chance?"

"Yes. That sounds like it."

"How terrible. Their father works—worked for Davidoff as his agent here. Are you sure he's dead?"

"Just from what the children say, I believe."

"Perhaps I should talk to them. Are they awake?"

"I'm sure I don't know, but we can see."

They moved out through the sitting room, where a passenger who was a doctor was examining a Japanese coolie with severe burns. In the passageway, people were lying on the carpet and sitting against the bulkhead. Some had burns and some had open, bleeding cuts. Many were bruised and scratched, and their clothes were torn, filthy,

✳ 98 ✳

and damp. There were Asiatics and whites, men and women, and there was a low undercurrent of groans and moans. Hannah was moving from one person to the next with a pitcher of water and a glass.

In the Hong Kong Suite, Dr. Holden had set up an emergency table and was working on someone lying on it when Wheeler and Robertshaw came in.

"Where are the children, Doctor?" Robertshaw asked.

Holden, his face darkened with a shadow of beard, his hair hanging down over his forehead, and a concentrated frown on his face, barely turned to them. "In there," he said, gesturing to the bedroom.

"Are they awake?"

"I don't know. Go on in."

Robertshaw knocked, and a woman's voice said "Yes? Come in." He pushed the door open and they moved in awkwardly.

"This man is from the British consulate, Miss Clare," Robertshaw said. "He would like to find out about the children."

Madelaine sat by the bed with Susan cradled in her arms asleep. Peter was on the bed, but he sat up quickly when the men came in.

"They're very tired," she said. "Can't it wait?"

"Just to know who they are, Miss," Wheeler said softly. "I believe I know the family. Yes, Peter it is you, isn't it?"

"Yes, Mr. Wheeler."

"Are you all right?"

"My arm was hurt, but the doctor fixed it."

"And Susan?"

"She doesn't understand, sir. She doesn't really know what happened. She's been crying a lot, but Miss Clare has been very nice to us and Susan is asleep now."

"What did happen?"

"Oh—" Madelaine started to protest.

✳ 99 ✳

Peter, his eyes big and beginning to fill with tears, looked up at Wheeler solemnly, then finally spoke, almost in a whisper. "They fell in."

Madelaine put her hand out to him. "It's all right, Peter dear. You don't have to say any more."

"I want to tell Mr. Wheeler," he said quietly. "He knows my Mummy and Daddy." He gulped and took a deep breath, then raised his head and went on. "Susan and I weren't right next to them. We were chasing those paper things that people were throwing from the ship, when everything started shaking and bouncing around. We both fell down, and when I looked back for Mummy and Daddy there was a big hole where they had been standing. Lots of people there fell in, I think." He stopped, his voice breaking.

"I see," Wheeler finally spoke quietly.

"Susan was crying and we didn't know what to do. My arm was hurt. We hid by the building to get out of the wind and the dust, and then the man from the ship came and took us up the gangplank and brought us here. They thought Mr. David...would take care of us, but he wouldn't let us in, so we came to this place."

"Thank you, Peter," Wheeler said. "It's been a terrible thing, and you've been very brave. I hope that you can get some sleep now. We'll talk some more tomorrow."

Before leaving, Wheeler spoke quietly to Madelaine. "Thank you very much. You're very good to do this. I was hoping there might be some clue that they survived. A lovely couple, friends of ours, but it sounds rather conclusive."

"I'm afraid so," she answered. "I hope they can sleep now. They're such dears."

"I'll check with you in the morning." He went out quietly.

He joined Robertshaw in the passageway.

"I don't know about any other family for those children. If I remember rightly, their grandparents are all dead.

Both the grandfathers were killed early in the war. I don't know about aunts and uncles." He paused, shaking his head. "Well, where should we start? Is there one place where survivors have gathered?"

"Most of them are in the second-class lounge," Robertshaw answered. "We can go there, and we can put out the word to have people report to you there. Those who can move."

While they were talking, Chin Ching came down the passageway toward the Hong Kong Suite, saw Robertshaw, and stopped. He turned and went back to where Mikaela's stretcher was just being brought around a corner from the elevator and motioned the bearers to halt. "Wait one minute," he said softly. "Wait till Mr. Lobbyshaw go."

Robertshaw saw the stretcher, and Chin Ching hesitated for a moment. Then he and Wheeler turned in the opposite direction. Chin Ching decided to head the other way toward officer's country. He would have to tell the captain that the Swedish lady was here before anyone else saw her, even the doctor and especially the staff captain, who might have noticed. Captain should know about Mr. Graham from the company, too.

When they got to the passageway where the officers' cabins were, Chin Ching had the bearers stop, and he ran on quickly to the bridge.

The captain was in the sitting room of his quarters, slumped in a chair with a hand over his eyes, but he snapped upright when Chin Ching came in. Chin Ching's smooth face never gave any clue about what he was thinking, and Sam felt a stab of fear at the news he might be bringing.

"Lady here," Chin Ching said quietly.

Sam started out of the chair and gripped the desk. "Where is she? Is she all right?"

"She hurt. Maybe bad, maybe no. I take to doctor, but

Mr. Lobbyshaw there so I bring her here first for you to see, you to tell where to go."

"Yes. Good. Good. Take me to her."

As they went down the bridge ladder, Sam said, "The pilot's cabin is vacant. Mr. Loomis has gone to the freighter. We'll put her in there for now. Get the key."

The stretcher was on the deck in the passageway with the bearers standing by when Sam and Chin Ching came to it. Sam stopped and she put one hand up toward him.

"Mikaela. Mikaela," he said hoarsely. "I've been out of my mind." He took her hand and held it tight. "Thank God. Thank God. You're here." He paused. "You're hurt. Is it bad?"

She nodded silently, her eyes brimming with tears. "Yes," she whispered. "But you saved me. You sent your man. I never would have gotten out."

They were both silent as he gripped her hand tightly. Their eyes held for a long moment.

"We'll see to it. We'll get the doctor for you. And you're here."

Chin Ching was back from the steward's board with the key to the pilot's cabin, a space used only when the pilot had to stay aboard because of rough weather when they left a port, or, as Loomis had done, when they went onto the next port to pick up another ship to bring back. The spread was damp and streaked with blood where Loomis had been lying down for a while, but Chin Ching pulled it off, and the sheets were clean.

With help from Chin Ching, Mikaela was able to slide onto the bed, giving one little yelp of pain that she quickly stifled. The stretcher crew left, and Chin Ching stood by the door silently.

"I'm an awful mess," Mikaela smiled weakly through her tears.

"But you're here." Sam smiled at her and took her hand again.

"I never thought I would get out until your Chin Ching came. And the other men came and had to help lift that awful piece of wood from me. And then we were attacked, and the shooting—" her voice trailed off.

"Attacked? Shooting?"

"Looters, Captain," Chin Ching put in. "Very bad on shore."

Sam gave her hand an extra squeeze and stood up by Chin Ching, taking him just to the door.

"A marvelous job, Chin Ching. I thank you. Who knows that Mrs. Swenson is here? Who were the men who helped you?"

"Mr. Perkins and men with him; Mr. Graham from office. He come down to boat. Just get away from building— all people there die but him. He come in boat. And Mr. Simms. He help Mr. Perkins on shore. Looters attack us, but guard from lifeboat come with gun and scare away."

"What a business," Sam said. "Well, I want Mrs. Swenson to stay here and be comfortable without any other people knowing. You understand?"

"Yes, Captain."

"And I want the doctor to come see her. Fetch him for me."

Chin Ching nodded and moved away quickly. Sam went back to the bed and took her hand again.

"It's a miracle," he said, "a miracle that you made it. You were back at your building?"

"Just walking in the door, or I would have been crushed. People near me were killed, and I was held down under a big piece of wood."

"And it's your leg that's hurt?"

"Yes."

"Anything else?"

"I don't know. I just hurt—all over. And I'm such a terrible mess. What is your awful English word? Pissed? I have pissed in my clothes, I know. And rats ran across me, and I was lying in wet dirt."

"We'll take care of you, my dear. None of that matters now that you're here." He paused, meeting her eyes. "I can't tell you what it was like when I couldn't come to you, and I was almost sure that you couldn't be alive. I..." He choked and lowered his head, holding her hand even more tightly. "You mean so much to me."

"I too," she said. "I thought, even if I lived, that I would never see you again. I was sure something terrible had happened to the ship. But you saved her, I heard the man say in the lifeboat."

"For now, yes. We got away from the flames, but we still have to get out of the harbor."

"It seems so peaceful here."

"Yes, for now, but the ship is in terrible shape and we have hundreds of survivors aboard. All sorts of problems."

"You shouldn't worry about me," she said.

"How can I not?" He looked into her eyes again.

Dr. Holden came to the door and knocked, and Sam stood up.

"You sent for me, Captain?"

"Ah yes, Doctor. I'm glad you could come. I know what you have been going through. This is Mrs. Swenson from the Swedish consulate. Chin Ching was able to rescue her from the wreckage of her flat. She has an injured leg and perhaps some other problems. She was trapped under a heavy piece of wood for almost twelve hours."

Lines of strain showed on Holden's face, with its stubble of beard, and his white coat was stained with blood in several places. Chin Ching stood behind him in the passageway.

"I'll have a look," Holden said, moving forward slowly.

"I must go back to the bridge, but I'll check with you shortly," Sam said as he left.

"Are you in pain?" Holden asked. He took Mikaela's wrist to feel her pulse.

"Yes, my leg," she murmured, "and almost all over from the wood holding me down. And I'm so dirty—"

"Of course. Don't worry. We'll get you clean as soon as possible. I know how you feel."

After taking her pulse and looking into her eyes to see if they were focused, he examined her leg as gently as he could. Standing straight, he sighed deeply. "I'm afraid you have broken your ankle. I hope that's all."

"I was sure," she said in a low voice. "It does hurt."

"To examine you more I will have to get these clothes off. They're certainly no good to you any more."

He gave a small apologetic laugh. "Normally a nurse would do it, but we don't have that luxury. I hope you don't mind a doctor doing it."

Her try at a smile was weak. "I am a Swedish woman. We are not easily embarrassed. But I am embarrassed that you will find I have not been able to control my bladder for all the time I was pinned there."

"That's understandable," he muttered. "It's not new to a doctor. I'll do what I can to get you clean. Let me know if I'm hurting you."

From his kit he took a pair of scissors and began to cut her clothes away, dropping them in the wastebasket. The cabin had a wash basin near the bunk, with towels, and when she was naked, he put a bath towel under her, moving her very cautiously, and then began to wash her body gently with hand towels, looking for other signs of injury as he did so. She lay quietly, with her eyes closed, shivering slightly when the damp cloth first touched her flesh.

He did his best to maintain a professional impersonality as he went about the task, but the sight of her magnificent body affected him. It brought back memories of his ex-wife and the struggles and battles they had gone through before breaking up, and of the months of unhappy celibacy since. And suddenly, the image of Madelaine Clare flashed before him, and the feel of her in his arms, when he had held her briefly in the cabin. She, too, would have a body like this.

To get hold of himself, he turned to rinse the towel, then decided to take a fresh one, tested the temperature of the water, and soaped it. Again she started when the dampness hit her flesh.

"I'm sorry," he said. "I don't mean to upset you."

"Oh, no. I am not upset. It's just a little shock to feel the water."

"We're making progress," he said soothingly as he continued the task, trying as best he could to shake the images from his mind.

"I think we have good news about other injuries," Holden finally said. "You have bruises, but I don't find anything worse. Do any other areas hurt? Your chest, your stomach?"

"Not really, but—" she hesitated. "But I would like to know something else. When you, when you cleaned me in my—my loins, I guess you say, was there any blood, or anything more than the mess my bladder made?"

Holden looked at her in surprise. "No. Are you menstruating now? Is that it?"

"No. Just the opposite. I am pregnant just a couple of months."

"Are you sure? Have you seen a doctor about it?"

"No. Not yet. I would be soon."

"How do you know?"

"I have missed two menstruations now, since June."

"And your husband? Was he here? Is he missing?"

"I have no husband. I am a widow."

"Oh." He stood in silence.

"I am glad," she said. "I want to keep the baby."

"This must have been a real strain for you. I think you are very lucky not to lose it, what you've been through." He shook his head.

"Please do not say anything to the cap—to anyone, please," she said. "I do not want anyone to know. Do you promise?"

"Of course. I'm a doctor." He smiled at her. "And meanwhile, I'll have to figure what to do about your leg. It will need setting, I'm afraid. We're not set up well to do that, but I will work something. I'll give you something for the pain in the meantime, so you can sleep."

He looked around the cabin and saw a bathrobe hanging on the back of the door. "Here, this is for you to wear for now." He helped her on with it carefully.

"I'm going to give you a shot to help with the pain in your ankle and to let you sleep. I will have to get another doctor to help me with your leg."

While he prepared the morphine shot, looking down at her supine body and the damaged leg, a sudden image came back to him of the rows of injured in the trenches. Her filthy clothes reminded him of the Flanders mud, and he shook involuntarily, pausing to get a grip on himself. As he was giving the shot, he heard voices in the passageway. The captain was coming back, talking to someone with him.

"How are we doing?" the captain asked quietly.

"It is a broken ankle, Captain. I'm giving her a shot to help with the pain, and she'll sleep. I will need help in setting it. One of the passenger doctors is a surgeon, I think. I'd like him to see it. Why Graham," he said in surprise, seeing who was with the captain. "You came through it!"

"By some luck," Graham said. "Only one in the office, I'm afraid. I can tell you it was some pleasant surprise to see the ship all lit up when I made it down to the harbor. I thought she must have been caught in it too."

"Are you all right?" Holden asked. "No injuries?"

"Cuts and bruises. One of the doctors down in the suites took care of me, and I came here to see the captain and to see how Mrs. Swenson is. She looked badly hurt in the lifeboat."

"Broken ankle, but nothing more. She'll be asleep soon. I've given her a shot."

"Good for you, Mikaela," Graham called in to her.

"Thank you George," she smiled weakly.

"Where would we be without the ship, eh?" said Graham. "Captain, you've done a marvelous job. I'd like to wireless the company what's happened. I know they'll be proud of what you've done. You've certainly earned your new command. Your wife will be so proud."

"Thank you, but you may be premature. We have tried to contact someone with our wireless, but we haven't been able to raise anyone on shore as yet," Sam said. "Perhaps tomorrow, and of course they will have to have the sad news about the office staff as soon as we can get it to them."

"Yes. It's terrible. Well, I'll let you sleep, Mikaela," said Graham. "I'll see what I can do to help down at the medical station. That's some scene there."

"I'd better get back too," Holden said. "I'll check again later. I hope you can get some sleep Mrs. Swenson." As he was leaving, the ironic thought struck him: opium derivatives were getting a workout. Paregoric and now morphine.

"Thank you Doctor." Her voice was already slurring.

Sam came and stood by the bunk, looking down at her. She raised her hand to him and smiled. "I feel so safe now, and I'm with you."

Sam winced inwardly at the word safe, but his face, set in deep lines, didn't show it. He held her hand silently until it fell limp, then he went to the bridge.

The night air was soft when Sam went to the rail at the wing of the bridge and looked out into the darkness. A breeze just beginning to stir in the quiet carried the awful stink of the ruined city. On the far horizon there was still a glow of distant fires, and he wondered how widely the earthquake had spread its devastation. Down on the water the ship's lights glinted on the sheen of the surface, a sign that they were still surrounded by oil from the ruptured storage tanks. The wake of a ship's boat returning from shore made small mounds on the surface instead of curling into foam. The water detail was still working with the people in the park. No more encounters with looters, he hoped.

Along the Bund, all was dark except for one flicker of fire at the east end. Around the harbor, some of the ships showed lights, and one or two lighters stranded along the shore were smoldering. Over all was a silence that he found ominous and eerie after the roaring terror of the afternoon, and he suddenly wished that he were far, far away. As inured as he was to the responsibilities of command, and as much as he usually enjoyed them and their routine, the *Monarch*'s situation now was the most overwhelming burden he had ever faced. That the murder of Davidoff meant comparatively little among the multiple problems of the ship herself and the confusion of coping with the refugees, was a shocking indication of the situation. He suddenly felt bone tired, his eyes still burned, and a terrible sense of helplessness made him sag against the rail. Perhaps, with the second mate now standing by on the bridge and Mikaela asleep, he should try to lie down for the few hours until dawn to be ready for the problems the next day would bring.

He called the mate over to him. "I'm going to try to catch up on sleep for a while, but I am to be called for any problem whatsoever. Take over, sir."

PART

III

H OLDEN, so tired that he stumbled occasionally, came into the Hong Kong Suite and found Dr. Osgood, one of the passengers who had volunteered to help, working on a casualty on the makeshift table. A tall, distinguished, white–haired man, Osgood was a noted bone surgeon, and Holden wanted him to see Mrs. Swenson's ankle. So as not to interrupt Osgood, he went quietly to the cabinets from his regular sick bay that had been set up on the far side of the room, against the verandah deck entrance. He was not sure which one had been the hiding place for the vodka; he only knew he needed it now to keep him going. There it was, on the back of a shelf in the second one he looked into. He quietly poured a slug into a paper cup and downed it. It helped.

When Osgood had finished what he was doing, Holden told him of the problem with Mikaela and said he would like to have it looked at.

"She's sedated now with a morphine shot. It might be a good time to do what's needed," Holden said. "She was trapped for twelve hours in wreckage, and one of the ship's boat crews found her and brought her aboard. The captain seems to have a special interest in the case."

"Well, let's see what we can do," Osgood answered.

"Are you all right, sir?" Holden asked. "It's been a long pull, and I certainly appreciate what you've been doing."

"Nothing like an old fire horse when the bell rings," Osgood smiled grimly. "Reminds me of war duty."

"Yes. I know," Holden said quietly.

Gathering bandage and splint material, they left together. Chin Ching was dozing in a chair in the corridor outside the pilot's cabin and started up when they appeared.

"We're going to see to the lady's leg," Holden told him. "Has she been quiet?"

"Yes. No noise. No talk."

Mikaela stirred and mumbled when they turned the light on but remained quiet otherwise. Osgood leaned over to examine the ankle.

After a long silence, he straightened. "A complicated one, I'm afraid. It's a surgery case, and I wouldn't want to do it here. We can splint it temporarily, but she must be operated on soon to save the leg."

"I was afraid of that," Holden answered.

Working together, they accomplished the splinting with an occasional murmur from Mikaela. "Best we can do now," Osgood said. "I wish it were more."

"We can look in on her in a few hours. I'm afraid she'll need another shot," Holden said. "I'm glad you were here. I don't get many broken bones in my duty here. Seasickness is my specialty." He gave an ironic laugh.

Turning out the light and closing the door softly as they left, Holden spoke to Chin Ching. "She should be asleep for a few more hours, Chin Ching. We've done what we can for now. Maybe you should get some sleep."

"I get little nap here sometimes. Captain trying to sleep now. He very tired."

"I can imagine. We're all that way," Holden said over his shoulder, walking down the passageway with Osgood.

"I don't know when we can get her to a proper hospital," Holden said. "I'm worried about her, and several other critical ones."

"It's going to be difficult," Osgood answered. "We'll do the best we can."

When they got back to the Hong Kong Suite, Holden decided that he would have to lie down, or he would be no good for all the problems that lay ahead. Another passenger, a Dr. Hoover, had come in to see if he could help, and Holden decided that it was a good time for him to take a break.

"Since you gentlemen are here, I think I will lie down before I fall down," he said. "I'm sorry, but I wouldn't trust myself to do the right thing unless I get a bit of rest."

"You're right," Osgood said. "Dr. Hoover and I will carry on for a while. You'll have a great deal on your hands tomorrow, I'm sure."

"Yes. That's what I'm afraid of. Thank you, and be sure to call me if there is any problem. An hour or two should do me."

He thought the second bedroom might be vacant, but he saw that both beds were occupied, one by Hannah. He went to the other door and moved in quietly. Madelaine Clare was lying on one bed, with Susan cradled in her arms and Peter next to them. There was a dim light from the desk, and he stood and looked down at them. Suddenly a lump came to his throat and tears stung his eyes. None of the terrible things he had seen all day had affected his professional approach, but this brought an emotion that was personal and very poignant. With her features composed in sleep, there was a calm beauty about Madelaine that touched him deeply, and the plight of the children became very real to him.

He was about to stretch out on the other bed when Madelaine stirred and opened her eyes.

"Oh. It's you," she said dimly. "Is something wrong?"

"No. I wanted to see if you were all right, and I think

I'll lie down for a while myself. I'm pretty tuckered out. How are you?"

"I guess I dropped off." She shook her head and sat up. "I'm—I've just been so worried about the children, and about all the injured people. Hannah and I have been trying to give them some comfort with drinks of water, and towels, and I've loaned some clothes to women who needed them. Some of them were almost naked, poor things." As she said it, her voice broke, and she began to sob. "I'm all right, but I'm so frightened."

He came to her and put an arm across her shoulder, feeling her shake beneath his touch.

"I'm just weak," she moaned, and buried her face against his jacket. He sat down on the bed to hold her less awkwardly, and she came into his arms fully, burrowing against his neck.

Talking didn't seem necessary, and he just made soothing sounds and patted her back until the sobbing slowed.

"Hold me tight," she whispered. "It feels so good."

"You'll feel better," he said lamely.

Making an effort, she raised her head and passed a hand across her eyes, trying to dry them. "I'm so glad you came," she said, then, hesitating she went on. "Would you think I'm crazy if I asked you to lie with me on the bed and hold me? I... it would mean so much to have you here."

"I understand," he answered. "Let's."

He took off his jacket and shoes and stretched out, and she came to him silently, nestling against him, with her head on his shoulder and his arm around her. She gave one great sigh, and in a very few minutes they were both asleep.

Robertshaw came back to his cabin in a highly nervous state after pausing on the deck to look at the smoldering fires along the shore. Fear stabbed at him, and his hands were shaking as he tried to turn the knob of his cabin door.

✳ 116 ✳

We should be away from here, he thought. Why are we still here? As we turned the corner of the corridor, could that have been the captain's woman friend on the stretcher with her blonde hair spilling over the edge and that slanty-eyed, sneaky Chinaman standing there? What did Applebye think he was doing, if in fact he had had her brought aboard? He should have gotten the ship out of here instead of worrying about some woman.

He found the cabin light switch after some groping with his shaking hand and looked around the room suspiciously, as though expecting danger there, then caught a glimpse of himself in the dressing mirror. His eyes were wide and staring, and there was a gathering of moisture under his nostrils. "Get hold of yourself," he muttered aloud, taking a deep breath and grasping the edge of the dresser to stop his hands from trembling. Steadying himself, he reached up to pat his breast pocket. Yes, the letter was still there.

Got to get some rest, he told himself. Tired; tired; must rest. He took off his coat, not bothering to hang it up as usual, kicked off his shoes and dropped to the bunk, leaving the light on. Somehow he didn't want to be in the dark. Closing his eyes, he tried to relax, but, in half-dreams, visions of flames leaped before him, mixed with the image of Chin Ching's impassive face as he lurked in the corridor, and the shine of the woman's hair. When he did drop off, his sleep was deeply disturbed and he would wake with a start, expecting to see flames outside the porthole, but it was only the black night.

There was a heavy knocking on the sitting room door. Sam struggled out of a deep sleep and a confused dream of Alicia and Julian urging him to do something .he couldn't. He was aware of the pungency of his sweat as he reached for his uniform jacket. He groped for his shoes and shouted "Yes, I'm coming."

"Captain, are you awake?" the second mate was calling, and Sam opened the door quickly.

"What is it?" Sam asked, stepping out to the bridge wing.

"There's a fire, sir, over on the shore." The mate pointed.

Through the murky haze of early morning a pillar of flame and smoke rose from the shoreline a few hundred yards east of the end of the ruined Customs pier. A light onshore breeze was blowing the smoke slowly inland. Sam took the binoculars from their rack and concentrated on the blaze, realizing as he did that his eyes still smarted.

"It's a wrecked lighter up against the beach," he said. "I think the flames will stay there with the breeze this way. We should keep an eye on it."

"Sorry to disturb you, sir, but I thought you should see it."

"Of course." Sam yawned and rubbed his eyes. "Is there anything in the teapot?"

"Yes, sir. Some. I'll send for more."

"Is Chin Ching about?"

"He was in the passageway at the pilot's cabin most of the night, sir. Shall I fetch him?"

"Yes. Please."

While the mate was gone, Sam kept an eye on the fire. If it stayed there in an onshore breeze, there was no problem, but he was very much aware of the oil slick on the water, surrounding the ship and stretching between her and the shore. If that ever caught...

With the dust and haze of the day before gone, the ruined city stood out starkly in its devastation. He was appalled at the sight of the total destruction everywhere he looked. The harbor was still full of wreckage and anchored small craft. Some had people aboard, and some seemed abandoned. The French liner *Renaissance* had dropped away from her berth at the end of the pier and was anchored several hundred yards off. Evidently her engines were not yet operative, or he was sure she would have moved to the outer harbor. She probably had kedged with her anchors to where she was now.

While he was scanning the scene, Chin Ching came out with a tray of rolls, fruit juice, and a fresh pot of tea.

"Chin Ching, how do you do it?" Sam marveled. "That's just what I need." He helped himself. "How are things in the pilot's cabin?" he asked when the mate had moved into the navigation table with his cup.

"She still sleep, Captain. Doctors come and fix ankle while she sleep from shot Dr. Holden give her. She have splint and bandage now."

"Good for them. I hope she stays asleep. What a terrible experience." He paused, then looked straight at Chin Ching. "And I thank you. You did a fine job, Chin Ching. I am very grateful."

Chin Ching bowed his head." Happy to do, Captain." Raising his head, he asked, "You want shower, Captain? Fresh clothes? I fix for you."

"Perhaps in a while," Sam said. "I can't leave here now. I want to watch that fire." Calling to the mate, he asked, "Are the boat crews all aboard—the ones taking the water to the park?"

"Yes, Captain. They belayed about an hour ago. They were all very tired. I guess it was rough on shore. They had to fight looter gangs a few times."

"I want to get out of here. We must have hundreds of refugees by now."

"Mr. Wheeler from the consulate has been taking a count, I believe. Mr. Robertshaw was working with him for a while, but he is sleeping now."

"Well, we all need it sometime. How about you? You must be ready. I can relieve you."

"Thank you, sir. I have been up all night."

Sam kept watching the fire, hoping that it would stay where it was. It was just the wrecked lighter that was burning, and it had not spread. Suddenly, there was a flare-up, with the smoke thickening and the flames roiling up in greasy-looking masses, followed by a whirling column of fire several hundred feet high, spreading out from the burning hull.

"It's got the oil," Sam cursed. Even with the onshore breeze, this was no place to be. Sam called back the second mate, who was just leaving the bridge. "No rest for the weary. The fire's gone bigger. We have to get out of here. Call the other officers, and we'll set the special detail for getting underway. I have to go back and talk to Loomis on the freighter."

Robertshaw came out of his cabin, unsteadily, rubbing his eyes. Sam told him to stay in charge on the bridge while he went aft. Robertshaw looked at him through narrowed eyes. "We'll have to move soon, Mr. Robertshaw. I'm going to work it out with Loomis on the freighter."

He hurried aft on the promenade deck, where figures were huddled asleep in the deck chairs, and called the watch on the *Cape Fear* when he arrived at the fantail. He was relieved to see that it was Christiansen.

"I'm glad you're here," he said. "We must move the ships before that new fire on the shore works its way out here. It's in the oil now. Can you call Mr. Loomis for me, the Hong Kong pilot. We'll have to talk."

"Yes sir, he is just inside. I will get him." Before he even left, Loomis hurried onto the deck and came forward.

"I thought I heard you, Captain." His bruises had discolored, and his face was swollen.

"Ah, yes, Mr. Loomis. Have you seen the fire making

along the shore? It's time for us to move away, as quickly as possible, and I must depend on you."

"We're ready."

"As you know, our port screw is fouled on your port cable, and I don't dare use my starboard screw with all this wreckage between the ships. If I lose it, we are finished. Your stern is in the clear, and I propose that you tow us out to the turning basin. We'll lash to you with more wire, and I think it's best if you slip your port cable so we can separate when we get out there. Do you agree to this?"

"I do. We're single-screw, so we may tend to starboard with you on our bow like this, but I think we can make it. We'll get to slipping the cable right now. I'll give you three blasts when we're ready to go. We don't have a wireless operator. He was killed on shore, or I would say we could keep in touch that way."

"We'll work it out. I think this is the best way. I'll stand by on the bridge until we hear your signal." Sam waved a salute and hurried back to the bridge, where he passed the word for the deck crew to rig the lashing from the *Monarch*'s quarter to the *Cape Fear*'s bow. The other officers had all appeared, looking haggard and unkempt from their night of taking water ashore, and Sam set them to their stations for getting underway, explaining the special circumstances.

"Mr. Barclay, you will see to the wire between us and the *Cape Fear*. Make sure we are properly secured, and that when the time comes we can cast off quickly. The *Cape Fear* will tow us toward the turning basin, and we will anchor temporarily.

"Mr. Perkins, you will take the small boat to free our bow line from the pier and then follow us out to the anchorage. That can be done right now."

"Aye, aye, sir," Perkins said, and left hurriedly.

While the others went to their stations, Sam took up the binoculars again to watch the fire on the beach. It was

an awesome sight. The flames had spread along the waterfront, feeding on the oil. No more survivors from there, Sam
thought, as the columns of fire whirled and soared high in
uneven bursts. The breeze was still onshore, but it was very
light, and he was afraid that the flames could probably eat
against it, feeding on the great spread of oil between the ships
and the beach.

He watched as Perkins and two seamen took the small
workboat to the pier and a seaman scrambled up to free the
bow line. Now it was up to *Cape Fear*, and he turned to put
the glasses on the men working on her bow to slip her port
cable. Each moment he expected to see them straighten up
with the task finished, but nothing happened. Now that his
bow line was off the pier, only the *Cape Fear*'s starboard
anchor was holding the ships in position, and he was afraid
that they would swing around.

"What the hell are they doing?" he muttered to
Robertshaw. "They should have done it by now."

"We may swing," Robertshaw said.

Watching tensely, they waited for what seemed endless
minutes as the fire continued to roar along the shore. At last
the *Cape Fear*'s crew gave a wave to her bridge, and her
starboard anchor started to come in. Her whistle gave three
blasts, and slowly the ships began to gather way.

"None too soon," Sam muttered. "Now we're dragging
their port anchor. I hope it doesn't foul."

Their way gradually increased, and as it did the ships
began to tend to starboard, unable to hold a straight course.
Completely at the mercy of *Cape Fear*, Sam gritted his teeth
in frustration and watched as the swing continued.

"God damn," Sam breathed. "The French ship. We
may not clear her."

"What can we do?" Robertshaw asked wildly.

"Watch and pray," Sam growled. "It's going to be
close."

As the linked ships gathered speed, their course straightened slightly, and the *Renaissance* loomed closer and closer. People on her bridge were staring in astonishment. The *Cape Fear* just cleared, ticking the *Renaissance*'s stern briefly, and then the two liners were alongside each other. There was a horrendous screech of tortured metal, and a series of uneven jolts as the *Monarch*'s hull raked along the other ship. Stanchions bowled over along the railing of the French ship, and there was an extra explosion of sound when one of her lifeboats that had been hanging outboard in davits shot up in the air, splintering apart and crashing onto her boat deck as it bounced off the next lifeboat.

Sam cringed, cursing—it seemed as though his bridge wing would catch on the *Renaissance*'s superstructure. But now the *Monarch*'s stern was clear of the other ship's quarter, and she pivoted slightly, swinging the bow out. Sam could have almost touched the other ship as the bridge slid by, but all of a sudden they were in the clear, and the lashed ships were backing through open water toward the turning basin. Sam kept an impassive face despite the inner churning. After the ships cleared, he thought wryly that such things as murder and collisions were just a minor part of the picture in this wild set of circumstances.

Through a call to Barclay at the stern, who was in direct contact with *Cape Fear*, Sam relayed a message to Loomis at a point several hundred yards beyond the *Renaissance*. The *Monarch* put down her anchor and as soon as she did, the *Cape Fear* cast off the towing wires and steamed out the breakwaters to the outer bay. It would have been impossible for the *Cape Fear* to tow her out through the breakwaters the way they had left the pier, as an accurate course could not be held and there were obstacles of every sort in the way: wrecked and abandoned coastal freighters and harbor craft, and rafts of floating wreckage. Still, Sam would have liked to have his bow brought around so that the *Monarch* would be facing the opening in the breakwaters. This would have made it easier for her to make her way out to open water once her engines and steering had been tested. Now, as she rounded to her anchor slowly, *Monarch*'s bow pointed east, across the harbor, and it would be a difficult maneuver to work her around to the proper heading and through the narrow gap between the breakwaters. The breakwaters themselves were now half submerged from all the upheavals of the earthquake, and the two little lighthouses marking each side of the entrance were tilting at crazy angles.

The first thing to do was to check out the condition of the starboard propeller and the rudder. Sam gave a great sigh of relief when the reports were that the screw was normally operative, but he was disturbed by the news that the rudder was partially blocked.

The port screw was still fouled, too, but Sam surmised that it was just with *Cape Fear*'s cable: The ships would not have moved as well as they did if the anchor were still attached and dragging, and the forces involved had certainly been enough to break it free. He hoped that this was so. Still, the drag of the cable alone was enough to keep the *Monarch* from swinging normally to the wind.

Now that things were calm for a moment, he suddenly realized how tired he was, and what a scruffy mess he felt. His uniform was rumpled and dirty, he had been soaked with sweat several times, and he needed a shave. He decided a quick shower, a shave, and a change of clothes were in order. If he looked as much of a mess as the rest of his officers, he would not be a figure to inspire confidence.

Chin Ching, reporting that Mikaela was still asleep, had another uniform ready. Sam stripped, took a quick shower, gulped a cup of tea, and began to shave. He was just toweling off the last of the lather when Barclay came to his door.

"Captain, better have a look at the fire. It's changed course and seems to be heading our way."

Putting his uniform on as quickly as possible, Sam went back to the wing of the bridge and reached for his binoculars.

The sudden movement of the ship woke Holden up, and, for a brief moment he was disoriented, wondering where he was. He ached all over, and his mouth was foul and dry. The softness of Madelaine's hair against his cheek made him aware, and, as he opened his eyes, he saw the little girl standing beside the bed, looking at them with wide, grave eyes.

"That's the way Mummy and Daddy sleep," she said. "Are you married too?"

Before he could say anything, Madelaine woke up with a little gasp, and sat up.

"Oh Susan. How are you dear?"

"I'm fine. Are you married?"

Madelaine laughed softly. "No dear. We were just keeping each other comfortable. Where's Peter?" She looked around the cabin.

"He's in the bathroom. I've been."

"That's good. Well, we'll have to find us something to eat, won't we?"

"Yes. I'm hungry."

Holden struggled up, rubbing his eyes.

"Wow! How long have we been out?" He looked at his watch. "After seven o'clock, and we're moving."

Just then, they felt uneven jolts and shocks and heard the sound of the ships crashing together. Looking out the porthole, they could see the stacks and masts of another ship right alongside, and the bumping and scraping continued.

"We're hitting another ship," Holden cried. "That's all we need."

As he spoke, the other ship disappeared and the noises

and jolts stopped. "Whew. I guess we're clear." He swung his feet off the bed. "Well, it's back to work for me, I'm afraid. I didn't mean to sleep this long."

Madelaine put a hand on his arm and smiled at him. "You needed it. And you helped me. Thank you for being so kind."

He gave her a wry grin. "Thank you. You're the first movie star I've ever slept with. I think I'd have preferred slightly different circumstances." Their eyes met, and they both smiled. "How are you feeling?"

"Better, thank you. Everything seems better in the daylight. Maybe we're getting out of here."

"At least we're moving. I don't know how."

"I'll see if Hannah can find us something to eat. She's been wonderful working with the stewards and doctors taking care of all these poor people, and she seems to be friends with the stewards. Susan's hungry, aren't you dear? And so am I."

"I'm going to get some clean clothes and come back. Then I'll have to see what the situation is. The volunteer doctors have been splendid. We couldn't have managed without them. I don't know how many hundreds of injured there are."

"It's a frightful job," she said. "I watched you working and you were marvelous."

"It's me duty," he said with an exaggerated Cockney lilt. "Just me duty." He gave her a short hug. "Take care, and I'll be back. You've inspired me." She kissed him quickly on the cheek.

Peter came out of the bathroom.

"Good morning, Peter," Madelaine smiled at him. "How are you this morning?"

"I'm all right," he said, doubtfully. "I washed myself. We're moving, aren't we?"

"Yes. We seem to be. And we hit another ship, but then we went by."

"I heard all that noise." He paused and looked up at her. "If we're moving, where are we going? Won't we be in Yokohama any more?"

"I really don't know. We'll just have to wait and see."

"I wonder where we're going to live," Peter said. He came to Madelaine and buried his face against her, and she hugged him tightly. Susan stood very still watching them.

No rest for the weary, Sam muttered to himself. At least he didn't smell like a billy goat any more. He trained the binoculars on the remains of the Customs pier, where the flames from the fire along the shore were beginning to feed on the oil in the water. There was a terrifying, eddying whirl to the white hot flames, topped by a cloud of smoke. There were several pools of fire that would subside for a while and then suddenly burst into explosions of flame and smoke as they met a new supply of oil. Evidently, ruptured pipelines on the pier were feeding more oil into the fires as they moved, and three or four separate fires were advancing.

As he watched, Sam felt a breath of breeze against his cheek from the direction of the land, and it carried a new smell of burning oil, backed by the stink of ruins from the city. The day was bright and sunny, but the new light breeze from the shore held a deadly menace, and he cursed to himself.

"We must get underway immediately," he said to Barclay, who had been standing beside him, anxiously watching the fires himself. "Set the special fire details, and get the anchor up right away." He went to the engine telephone and advised them to be ready for full ahead very quickly. Steam had been kept at the ready ever since noon the day before.

The area around the *Monarch* was cluttered with floating rafts of wreckage, and small coastal freighters and schooners, evidently abandoned, were anchored all around her. He would have to try to avoid them, if only to keep his starboard propeller from fouling. As he watched the flames advance unevenly across the harbor oil slick, he realized that it was going to be a very near thing to get the ship across the path of the fires before they reached her. To bring her around to head out the entrance between the ends of the breakwater would require a great amount of backing and filling that would take much too long. The only hope was to go straight ahead across the turning basin to the southeastern corner of it, which was slightly to windward of the flames. As he watched the anchor detail on the bow, and the slow, link by link ascent of the chain, he gauged the advance of the nearest fire storms. He was not at all sure that they could do it in time. All our efforts so far, he thought, won't mean a thing. He was acutely conscious of the thousands of people in his care who trusted that they were in the safest place in Yokohama. All would be lost to the great whirlpools of fire creeping across the water toward them, pushed by the increasing land breeze.

A vision swept through his mind of what it would be like on the ship if she were engulfed in flames. He remembered the sight of ships that were torpedoed in wartime convoys suddenly erupting as a great ball of fire, and how he had imagined the horror of being caught that way. He had tried to think what he would do in such a case, realizing soon that there was nothing that could be done for the ship or those on board. There was no point in getting the lifeboats ready. If the flames reached them, the boats would be useless, and there were now far more people aboard than the lifeboats could handle. Again, the image of flames sweeping up the sides of the hull and across the decks, of lifeboats catching fire on their davits, of people jumping overboard through the flames only to land in the white-hot pool of fire on the surface, raced through his mind. It would make the *Titanic* disaster look like a picnic. Helplessly, he watched the deadly slow retrieval of the anchor. Never before had the windlass seemed so slow.

"Have the fire details alerted to starboard, Mr. Barclay," he ordered. "They won't be needed to port."

"Aye, aye, sir," Barclay answered. "They're all set. I—I don't know what they can do, but they are ready."

"I'll admit it's not much of a chance," Sam answered. "We have to get moving. That's the only thing that will save us."

Checking to windward on the progress of the separate pools of fire, he watched in horror as the nearest one off the starboard quarter moved toward a small coastal schooner that had been anchored between the *Monarch* and the shore. Its progress was like a great bellows. As a tongue of flame found a new patch of oil on the surface, it would leap out with a hissing roar and then would slow down and intensify. Between the surface and the flames there was a band of shimmering white heat that distorted everything behind it. One of these advancing fingers of new fire came between the *Monarch* and the schooner, which seemed to waver and flicker in odd distortion; then suddenly it caught fire. A ring of flame raced around the hull behind the weird curtain of heat, and in no time the vessel was a great pillar of sparks that blended with the oil flames into a towering scarlet pyre.

"Good God," Sam breathed. "I hope no one is still aboard her. That one should pass astern of us, but the big one off the starboard beam is the one we have to watch."

He didn't voice it, but the thought was all too strong in his mind of what kind of mountain of flame the *Monarch* would make if she were caught, if the little schooner could go up in such a spectacular burst. Once again he turned to check on the progress of the anchor detail. To the other officers on the bridge, his strong features, steady blue eyes, and the deep lines around his mouth seemed the picture of confident calm, but he seethed inside.

Perkins, with the anchor detail on the bow, watched the chain's painfully slow ascent, then looked out to starboard just as the big pool of fire there caught a new supply of oil and erupted skyward in a great roar. The flames just off the water were white and thin, then swirled higher into thick black smoke, and the sound was a terrifying tumult. Already he could begin to sense heat from the fire against his cheek, and he suddenly felt a return of the panic he had known during the typhoon in Hong Kong. Leaving his station, he dashed to a forecastle companionway nearby, with its protective hooded shelter, and cowered against the steel. Grasping the handrail tightly, he was overcome by trembling. After a while, he heard the bosun shout, "Anchor's aweigh," and realized that he should be making the report. Shocked to his senses, he came back out on deck and made the hand signal up to the bridge. No one, he hoped, had seen what had happened but he saw the bosun looking at him oddly. Shaking and bathed with sweat, he checked that the crew was securing the anchor properly, and he felt the surge of the ship beginning to move.

As soon as Sam got the word from the foredeck, he signalled for full speed ahead on the starboard propeller, gave the helmsman a heading that would take the ship diagonally across the path of the advancing fires, and then had nothing to do but stand and watch, taking visual bearings all the while as the ship gradually gathered way. His main hope was that the cable on the port propeller would not hold her back too much, and that the anchor on it had been lost. He watched the helmsman carefully to see how the steering was going. He seemed to be able at least to keep her on a straight course.

Now he concentrated on the great whirlpool of fire off the starboard beam. It was towering ever higher, feeding on a new patch of oil on the surface, and it seemed to be heading right for the ship. The other pools of fire were not close enough to threaten them—this was the one they had to beat. Inch by inch, he noticed, the bearing was drawing aft, but if a stronger gust of wind increased its speed, they probably would not make it. Under the strange circumstance of the fouled port screw and the dragging cable, he had no way of accurately telling how the ship would move. For a moment he began to plan what they would have to do if the flames did reach them, but he had no picture of how to handle it. It was too hopeless a mess to think clearly about; instead he concentrated on the bearing. If it did come, the hoses were ready. That was all that could be done. Already he could feel the heat from the flames on his cheek.

As the fire storm advanced, it engulfed a raft of floating wreckage, which, like the schooner, flared high in bright scarlet, increasing the heat. This spread the area of flame and made it more difficult to gauge the bearing, but now Sam could feel the motion of air from their forward progress. The ship was gathering way well. Maybe...maybe...It did seem now as though they were gaining—the bearing was definitely drawing aft. He looked back at the wake and saw a satisfying swirl churning away from the starboard screw. She was going faster now.

Barclay, Robertshaw, and the quartermaster on watch had all been standing silently, doing their own calculations on the advance of the flames. Now Barclay muttered quietly, "I think we've done it."

"I agree, Mr. Barclay," Sam said softly. "We seem to be clear."

The ship was headed for shallow water in the southeast corner of the bay, beyond the turning basin. Now, while the deadly pillar of fire passed beyond their stern by about 400 feet, it became a question of stopping the ship's advance before she ran aground. Sam signalled full astern on the starboard engine and ordered the anchor dropped again. While this was going on, they all looked aft at the path of the fire, which swallowed up two more abandoned coastal craft in great dazing bursts, then swept across the exact spot where the *Monarch* had been anchored twenty minutes before, with flames roaring several hundred feet into the air.

"Just as well we moved," Sam said dryly. "What next?"

The *Monarch* rounded to her anchor, and the flames gradually subsided as they ran out of surface oil. Their path had taken them between the *Monarch* and the *Renaissance*, which could be seen safely in the anchorage where the two ships had collided. *Monarch* was out of the path of the flames, but she was still in an untenable position in the inner harbor, where more fires could be expected.

"All we have to do now," Sam said to Barclay and Robertshaw, "is to get out to the outer bay somehow. Where the hell are any tugs? If we only had tugs to turn us it would be easy, but I guess we'll have to do it ourselves. I'm certainly not going to stay here very long."

Simms, asleep in a deck chair on the starboard side was awakened by jolting and crashing and the noise of metal against metal. He was startled to see the superstructure of another ship, just over the railing, sliding by.

"What the hell?" He sat up and watched in amazement while the *Monarch* jolted along. There was an extra loud crash as a lifeboat on the other ship exploded from the impact and crashed down onto the deck in a shower of wreckage. As his eyes and brain cleared, he realized that the *Monarch* was moving, not the other ship, which he now recognized as the *Renaissance*, and that *Monarch* was going astern. After a few more crashes, *Renaissance* slipped from view. Simms got up and went to the rail to see what was going on. He ached in every joint, and grunted in dismay at the condition of his clothes. Gradually he got his bearings, saw on his watch that it was 0730, and realized that *Monarch* was being towed by the stern by the freighter they had been lashed to during the night. They seemed to be headed for the turning basin, not the harbor entrance. At least they were away from the pier area. He looked back and saw the fire on the shoreline next to the pier. Good show to get out of there, no matter how, he thought. Looking over the side, he saw the sheen of oil on the water, and the ironic thought came to him that his former employer had lost a lot of his product. The harbor, he knew from his long experience with fueling ships, was a fire box waiting to ignite. He wondered what Captain Applebye had in mind for getting out of here. Perhaps he should have stayed on shore after all. This looked very dicey.

A Chinese steward was scurrying along the deck with an armful of sheets, and Simms called to him. "Any place for food? Where are people eating?"

"Second-class dining room," came the hurried answer as the man kept moving.

Simms found his way there after a stop in the men's room and joined a long line at the entrance to the dining area. It was a bedraggled, motley lot in every kind of garment, some obviously borrowed from passengers, some in the torn, filthy clothes in which they had come aboard. There were Europeans, Japanese and other Orientals; men, women and children. A few who seemed to have clean clothes of their own were obviously passengers. There was very little talk and no laughter or bantering—just a stoic acceptance of the situation and a patient numbness while the line moved slowly past serving tables that held juice, fruit, rolls, tea, and coffee. Once served, people moved to any seat they could find and ate silently while stewards moved through the crowd removing used plates as soon as someone was finished. Simms marveled at the orderly organization in the midst of general chaos and wondered wryly what the passengers expecting luxury and service were thinking of their lot.

While he was drinking his coffee, a young assistant purser came up to him. "Have you checked with the consul, sir?" he asked.

"No. Should I?"

"Yes sir, if you please. Mr. Wheeler from the British consulate is taking a census of all refugees aboard so as to compile an accurate report. He is located in the Yokohama Suite. We would appreciate it if you would check with him."

"Yokohama Suite?" Simms raised his eyebrows. "Where is that?"

"Starboard side, boat deck, sir. The medical station is also there if you need any medical attention."

"I guess I'll live. What's a few bruises between friends?"

"You will check in?"

"Right. Soon as I finish here, I'll do that."

"Thank you, sir." The purser went on around the room checking with all who were obviously refugees. Simms put his cup down and moved out, finding his way to the suite area. Several people were sitting against the bulkhead in the passageway between the suites, evidently waiting for a doctor to look at them, and, as he hesitated at the door to the Yokohama Suite, he could see more people milling about inside. Wheeler was behind a small table taking names and information from the people checking in. When Simms' turn came, Wheeler smiled broadly at him and shook his hand.

"Martin Simms! I'm glad to see you. Had no idea you were aboard."

"I was on the pier when the thing hit, so I popped up the gangplank," Simms said. "Better here than caught under some pile of bricks."

"I should say! Quite a time for you," Wheeler said, "with the change in your company, and now this."

Simms nodded in agreement. "Not much left of the

company now, I wager. Most of their inventory seems to be spread around the surface of the harbor and catching fire."

"Are there fires? I haven't had a chance to look out with all this to do. I do see that we're moving, at least."

"Seems the *Cape Fear* is giving us a tow. We'd better get out of here, all right. Whole harbor's likely to be ablaze before too long. If you're making a list, it may be of all the people lost when the ship burns up. Won't be much use to that, will there?"

"God, man, don't be so cheerful. Captain Applebye's done a fine job so far."

"That he has, but it could be that no man can save this ship if the burning oil catches her."

Wheeler stared back at Simms solemnly and finally spoke. "Well. Let's hope for the best. Between God and Captain Applebye perhaps we'll make it."

"By the way," Simms asked him, "I understood this was to be the suite of the lovely chap who put me out of business. What's happened to him?"

"Mr. Davidoff? Yes, this was his suite, but they moved him out before I got here. I don't know where he's gone."

"Well, I don't want to see him," Simms grumbled. "Am I officially a refugee now, Mr. Wheeler?"

"Yes, thank you. I'm trying to get all the names on board to transmit to the consulate in Kobe. There must be terrible concern among relatives and friends over what has happened to people here."

"Well, nobody has to be told about me," Simms said. "I'm on my own—though where, I don't know." He turned and went out the door.

Stratford, who had had about two hours sleep, put on a fresh uniform and managed to look composed and in control as he came to the bridge to confer with the captain.

"Captain, if you have the time now, Mr. Wheeler, Mr.

Robertshaw, Mr. Graham, and I would appreciate it if you could come with us on an inspection of the ship. I know how busy you have been on the bridge, but I thought this might be a good time for you to see the medical stations, the food arrangements, and some of the other things we have done."

"I agree with you Mr. Stratford," Sam answered. "I want to do it, but I hate to leave the bridge while we're still in such a tight place." He looked at his watch. "Perhaps if we do it quickly this would be a good time, but we must get the ship to the outer harbor as soon as possible. I have the wireless trying to contact tugboats to help us. While they're doing that I suppose I can do what you ask, though I'm sure you and your staff and the doctors have done a fine job."

"It's been very difficult, Captain, but everyone has been most helpful, and the passengers have been superb. They have formed an informal relief committee to help us in our work, and it would be most welcome if you could say a few words to them. I've asked them to meet in the smoking room in fifteen minutes."

"Well, let's get it done then," Sam said briskly, and he started off the bridge with Graham, Robertshaw, and Stratford. "Send for me if there is any problem, Mr. Barclay," Sam said as he left. "I will be back within thirty minutes at the most. I hope we have word from the wireless on tugboats by then."

Their first stop was the suite area on the boat deck, where they picked up Wheeler. Sam had a brief chat with Doctors Holden, Osgood and Hoover, who reported on roughly how many people they had treated—over 250. While they were in conversation in the Hong Kong Suite, the bedroom door opened and Madelaine came out, holding Peter and Susan by the hand.

"Oh, excuse us," Madelaine hesitated. "We were just going to get some air on deck for a few minutes. The children have been in the cabin a long time now."

"Ah, yes," Sam smiled at them. "It's a bit nicer than yesterday now, and we hope to be out in the bay very soon. We appreciate your cooperation and help, Miss Clare. It is very kind of you."

"Thank you, Captain." She gave him a tremulous smile. "It's been so awful for so many people. We just want to help all we can. The children have been very good. This is the captain, Peter and Susan."

They stepped forward shyly, with Peter giving a small bow from the waist and Susan a little curtsy. Sam felt a lump come to his throat as he smiled down at them.

"I'm glad you are well taken care of, children," he said. "Thank you again, Miss Clare."

Wheeler, Graham, Stratford, and Robertshaw started out the door, and Sam stepped close to Holden for a moment. "Any change? Any news?"

"Still asleep, Captain. It's a difficult break."

"I'll be back on the bridge in thirty minutes. Please check with me later," Sam said quietly, following the others out.

In the smoking room a group of men stood when the captain arrived. Sam recognized some of them from previous trips as prominent businessmen. He acknowledged those he had met before as he was quickly introduced by Stratford. Their spokesman, president of a large California bank, thanked Sam for coming and explained what they were doing.

"We are very impressed with the work everyone on this ship has done to help the refugees in this terrible catastrophe, Captain, and those of us you see here have banded together informally to do what we can to help. We have been collecting clothing from the passengers, who have been most cooperative. Some of us went ashore as volunteers with your water parties, and we helped to rescue refugees and bring them back to the ship. As you know, doctors from the passenger list have been helping take care of those who need medical help, and our wives have been trying to do what they can in passing food and water to the injured people, helping as what you might call nurses' aids, and providing clothing. We...we just want to pitch in in every way we can, and if there is something you would like us to do, please let us know."

Sam paused in silence for a moment, looking around at each one of them. "Gentlemen, I'm touched and impressed. I cannot thank you enough for this wonderful spirit of cooperation. We couldn't take care of this tremendous influx of refugees with just the ship's personnel, and what you are doing means a great, great deal. I have been so busy on the bridge that I have had to leave the organization of all this to my officers. I even forgot that this is Sunday, when I usually hold a religious service. We have stocked the ship for the ten-day passage to Vancouver, so we have plenty of food for the moment if we are careful with it.

"I must warn you that the ship is still far from clear of trouble, and I must be on the bridge most of the time, but I feel much better knowing that you are carrying on this way. Mr. Graham is representing the company, Mr. Stratford and Mr. Robertshaw are your contacts with the ship, and Mr. Wheeler is administering the relief work for the refugees. I can't tell you how much I appreciate what you are doing."

He shook hands all around again, with a word of thanks to each man, and the inspection tour continued. They took in the dining areas, the washrooms, and the lounges, where many of the refugees were lying on blankets. There was a heavy reminder of humanity, of sweat and dirty clothes, but the stewards were constantly policing trash and litter.

On their way back to the bridge, Wheeler spoke to Sam. "Captain, I have had several inquiries about Mr. Davidoff. I gather we are using his quarters, but I have not seen him. Do you know where he has moved?"

"I'm afraid I do not. He was not cooperative at all when we told him we needed the suite for emergency services, but we finally made him move. He's not a very sociable type, and I would suppose he is keeping to himself, wherever he is. He was the only person the Bridgeman children knew, but he refused to take them in."

"Sounds like him, from what I've heard," Wheeler said. "Well, I was just curious because people have asked me. Since he is on the passenger list, I don't have to include him on my list of refugees."

"No. That's right. Right you are," Sam answered. "I'd be happy if I never saw the chap again." With his stomach tightening, he hoped that his face showed nothing of what he was feeling.

He didn't dare look at Stratford in case the purser had overheard, and he realized that Robertshaw had been listening. Blast Davidoff. There were many more important things to do than worry about that unpleasant bastard, murder or no murder. He would have to face up to it sometime, but this was not the time.

When he got to the bridge, Barclay reported that there had been no response to the wireless calls for tugboat help. Communications were still garbled, with a great deal of local traffic, and shore stations were not in commission as far as could be told.

Sam looked over the situation. The turning basin was calm, and the sun was bright and pleasant. It was hard to imagine what it had been like about twenty-two hours ago. There were no surface fires at the moment, though there were some plumes of smoke along the shore by the Bund. The breeze was light from the east, and the ship was lying to it, so that her course to the entrance between the now sunken breakwaters half a mile away was ninety degrees to the left of her heading. Between the *Monarch* and the entrance there were a few rafts of wreckage, and one or two anchored small craft that had not been caught in the pools of fire. He would have to try to maneuver the ship past them and out through the entrance with no help, because he was absolutely sure that they could not stay where they were. It was just a matter of time before more oil leaked out into the harbor and more fires fed on the spill. Tugs or no tugs, blocked rudder or no, he would have to maneuver the ship. At least the wind was in the right direction to help him, and the operative starboard propeller was on the right side to make the ship turn to port. If the breeze held, he might be able to do it. He thought back on the mad dash across the advancing flames that got them where they were. If the breeze had been a point more in the south, the ship would have been caught in the whirlpool of deadly fire. Would it hold now to help the great ship turn? He had never had to handle a ship, especially a great hulking one like this, under such a handicap.

He ordered the anchor weighed and put the engine room on standby. When the anchor chain finally clanked its laborious way on deck and the "anchor's aweigh" signal was given, he called for slow ahead on the propeller and watched the bow anxiously to see if it would swing to port. The helmsman reported that the wheel would not go over for a left turn on the rudder, and Sam realized that the cable fouling the port propeller was probably blocking the rudder as well. If the ship did not swing to port, but just went straight ahead, she would soon be aground in shallow water east of the turning basin. If she fell off to starboard and the wind got on her port bow, she would be trapped in the basin with no way of coming around to the heading of the entrance.

Holding his breath, and concentrating as he never had in his life, he watched the bow against the shoreline for an indication of its movement. Finally, very gradually, it began to swing over to port. Now the breeze was on the starboard bow and helping the turn, but he couldn't let her swing too fast or too far, or she would be headed below the entrance, and he would never be able to get her to turn back up to starboard. When the swing became more pronounced, and the ship was making headway, he called for a burst astern on the screw. He repeated the same maneuver several times, balancing the forward motion with the swing of the bow, and keeping the heading just to the east of the opening between the breakwaters, so that the last swing would bring her into the slot. The tiny lighthouses, tilting crazily, were the only markers for the opening, because the breakwaters themselves had disappeared, evidently subsiding from the effects of the earthquake. Maybe there would be new shoals and new deeps in the area, differing from the charts after the great upheaval. That was a new thought, but he brushed it away. Since there was no way of telling, he would have to go ahead as best he could.

With the entrance coming closer, he spotted a large raft of wreckage off the port bow. If he let the bow swing below it, he would be below the entrance, and if he tried to come more to starboard by backing the screw in a sharp burst, it might be too big a turn afterwards to come down to the entrance.

"Wreckage to port, Captain," Robertshaw called nervously.

"I see it, thank you. We'll have to go through it." He felt the same way he had when he had ordered the full-speed-astern escape from the pier the day before, knowing they would be smashing into the *Cape Fear*. It was against all his instincts to take these actions, but there was no choice. He gritted his teeth and watched as the big spread of wreckage came under the bow and began to crunch along the hull. There were great pier pilings, wrecked lighters, and small, half-sunk harbor craft all in a tangled jumble, and the noise of it all grating along the waterline, with logs snapping and shooting their ends up, and the small boats twisting and turning over, was sickening to him. At least it was not to starboard, or they might very well be finished.

The mass of stuff, separated now, spinning and rolling, finally slid past the stern, and he breathed just a bit easier, with his eyes again on the approaching entrance. He hoped that the subsidence of the breakwater had not put rocks out into the channel, as he was quite close to the eastern edge. Another threat to the starboard screw!

Fortunately, the entrance was clear of other craft, as it would have been impossible to stop, or to avoid another vessel in the narrow slot. He gave a final order for a touch forward and then stop to bring the ponderous hull through the gap to the outer harbor. There was a thump and a scrape under the bridge as he looked down almost directly onto the eastern lighthouse, and he realized that some rocks must have tumbled off the breakwater during the quake. A quick order for a burst of reverse and an immediate stop was all he could do to give a slight swing to the stern away from the obstruction. Slowly the lighthouse slid aft, the stern did kick just a bit to port from the short reverse, and he breathed a great sigh when all 615 feet of her slid past without another jolt.

They were outside, but a look ahead posed even more problems. The outer anchorage was crammed with all sorts of vessels that had made their way out from the holocaust of the inner harbor. They were anchored close together, and there was no clear path to the open waters of Tokyo Bay beyond, where he dearly longed to be. On her present heading, the *Monarch* would end up in shoal water on the northwest side of the bay. In a mile, she would be hard aground. The course to safety was about two points to starboard, and he knew there was no way that the starboard propeller could be made to turn the ship those twenty-five or so degrees, especially into the wind with the fouled cable still dragging on the port screw. The only choice would be to go ahead for a few hundred yards, anchor, and then try to get assistance in turning his bow enough to the eastward to get to open water.

As he pondered this problem, he saw a harbor tug coming toward the entrance from the outer bay. This was one of the tugs that had been alongside when they were due to sail the previous day. She had fled the scene, and ever since they had not been able to raise her by wireless directly, or through other ships in the vicinity. Sam had a low opinion of the way the tug had acted, but he hoped now that this would be the saving instrument for the dilemma he was in. With his quartermaster frantically waving his signal flags for attention, Sam took his megaphone to the port rail and hailed the tug as loudly as he could. For a while the little vessel charged on unheeding, but, just under the bridge, she slowed down.

"Will you please take our tow line and pull our bow around to starboard," Sam bellowed. "We cannot turn by ourselves. Our rudder is jammed."

He turned to Barclay, who was standing beside him. "The buggers understand English when you are paying them for the job. I hope she hears me now. This is our answer if she will do it."

The tug made a turn, smoke belching blackly from her tall stack and came up along the port bow, where the bosun passed down a towing wire. The wire was made fast to the tug's towing bitts on her stern, and she started ahead and to starboard across the *Monarch*'s bow.

"God, no — the fool!" Sam cried. "She's turning too soon. She'll hang up doing that." He put the megaphone to his mouth but realized that he would never be heard at that distance. "She's got to go out dead ahead first and get us moving, then start us turning. Watch this," he groaned.

As he had predicted, when the tug, moving out on the starboard bow, took a strain on the towing wire, she was immediately twisted back into the *Monarch*'s bow and drawn in alongside. Sam raged in disgust. "How can a professional tug end up doing that? Her skipper must not be aboard."

While they watched in resignation, the tug cast off the line and steamed away through the entrance with no further communication.

"Well, we'll have to go ahead on this course and anchor until we can get some proper help." Sam's shoulders dropped, and he sighed. "We probably would have trouble maneuvering through all that gang of vessels anyway. We should be fairly secure out here for now."

"Let's hope so," Barclay said.

Proceeding slowly, with the forward and reverse alternations of the propeller keeping her fairly well on one heading, the *Monarch* moved across the outer harbor, barely skinning by a small, anchored freighter, until she reached an open spot large enough to accommodate her, some half a mile from the shoals off to the northwest. Sam gave the order to drop the anchor, and the ship came to rest on the same heading, with the dragged cable keeping her from swinging. The breeze had dropped off to a whisper, and the water was calm.

"Let's hope for the best," Sam muttered to Barclay.

When he went back to his cabin, he found Holden and Dr. Osgood waiting for him.

"We've had another look at the ankle, Captain," Holden reported.

"How is she?"

"She's still out, and I trust she's all right, but the ankle is a serious problem." He turned, deferring to Osgood.

"It's a compound fracture, Captain—a serious break. It will take an operation to do the needed setting and reconstruction, and I wouldn't dare to try it aboard here without the proper equipment," Osgood said. "If it isn't tended to fairly soon, there could be the danger of infection. Will the ship be going to another port soon?"

"I wish she were," Sam answered. "Right now we are stuck here with a fouled screw and no steering." He paused, deep in thought. "Are there other serious cases aboard? I'm sure there must be."

"About a dozen, Captain," Holden answered. "We have had one woman die of burns so far. We can take care of the burns in most cases, but we are just not set up to do operations, as you know."

"Perhaps we can work a transfer," Sam said, "or we just might get our screw and rudder in operation if we can find a diver. The naval base at Yokosuka just down the bay might have divers available, and we could then go on to Kobe, if we could get the work done. Mrs. Swenson has no other injuries besides her ankle?"

"She has bruises and minor cuts, but she came through it remarkably well, considering. I was afraid about internal injuries when I heard she had been pinned by a piece of timber, but there don't seem to be any."

"Well, we'll just have to keep her comfortable and hope for a solution very soon," Sam said. "I thank you both, and I trust you will continue to keep an eye on her. Are you keeping her sedated?"

"When she wakes up now, it might be a good idea for her to have a little something to eat. Then we can give her another shot before the pain becomes too severe again," Osgood answered.

"Well, thank you again," Sam said. "Are you still very busy with the refugees? There must be all sorts of problems."

"I think we've seen most of them," Holden answered. "Dr. Osgood, Dr. Hoover, and some other passengers have been a great help. I don't think there is anyone who has not been seen at least once. Of course we have to keep going, but it's mostly a matter of clean dressings and medication now. Women passengers have pitched in as nurses. It's remarkable how much everyone has helped."

When they had gone, Sam looked at his watch. It was just past noon. He was amazed to find that the whole morning had passed in the maneuvering away from the pier and out of the turning basin. Before he had time to think further, Chin Ching appeared silently with a sandwich and tea, and Sam sat at his desk to gather his thoughts while he ate. The ship was not clear yet. She could still be trapped by another fire, as there were still pools of oil all through the area, and it was not a secure anchorage if a strong breeze came up from the south. All the anchored vessels around them would make maneuvering under the starboard propeller almost impossible, and he couldn't go anywhere as long as the bow tended to the northwest. Through it all, the thought of Mikaela's situation remained, nagging at him. If only they could get away to Kobe where she could be treated in a well-equipped hospital...

Finishing his lunch, he decided to go to the wireless room to see what could be worked out there. "Sparks" was a wiry little Cockney, and there was a two-day stubble of beard on his narrow face and an overflowing pile of cigarette butts in his ashtray when Sam walked in, meeting a strong whiff of sweat and old cigarette smoke. Graham was there, anxiously looking over the radioman's shoulder as he tapped away at his key and fiddled with dials. Sparks looked up at the captain as he entered but did not rise; he kept at his key, a frown of concentration on his face and earphones on his head.

"Traffic's all jammed up, Captain," Graham said. "Very hard to make contact anywhere, but we've raised the *Cana dian Monarch* just offshore, inbound from Vancouver, and she seems to be able to get through to the British consulate in Kobe. She's been diverted there. We're just getting a message back now, I think."

Sparks was scribbling away on a message blank and Sam could faintly hear the squeaky jumble of dots and dashes in his earphones. He finished up with procedure signals and leaned back in his chair, removing the earphones.

"Ere you are, Cap'n," he said as he handed over the sheet. "Can you read it, or should I type it?"

"I think I can make it out," Sam said, frowning over the piece of paper and reading aloud.

Congratulations to Captain Applebye for saving ship. Well done. Vessel is to remain in Yokohama area until further notice as official relief station for evacuees in area. Please report number of refugees aboard. This is official order from Home Office. Signed H. Selwyn-Jones, British Consul.

Sam stood in silence, then turned to Graham. "I guess he doesn't know his official relief station may need a little relief herself. There may be nothing left at all unless we get the screw and rudder clear. Wish I could draw him a chart of where we are." He paused. "How does he know I saved the ship, anyway?"

"I believe Mr. Wheeler sent a wireless a short while ago, when we passed through the breakwaters, Captain. It will be difficult, I know, but this is a great honor for C & O and I'm sure much good will come of it."

Sam stared at him for a moment. "I hope you're right, Mr. Graham. I hope you're right. It's not going to be easy."

Sparks lit another cigarette and leaned back, sighing quietly, then sat up again as the radio crackled to life in the earphones. He picked them up and once more started to copy, frowning and asking for repeats once or twice. When he finished he handed the sheet to Sam.

"It's from H.M.S. *Masai*. She's a tribal class destroyer," Sam said. "She's at Yokosuka on a courtesy visit, I was told yesterday." He started to read.

Advised by Loomis of *Cape Fear* that you have fouled propeller and rudder and many casualties. Believe can arrange local navy dive team to examine and possibly clear same tomorrow. We may be moving casualties to Kobe. Please advise condition and location.

Sam turned to Graham with a small grin. "Well, speaking of the devil, or angel, or something. Good old Loomis. He didn't forget us."

"My! That's marvelous," Graham cried. "Do you suppose they can do it?"

"They can only try," Sam answered. "You may have heard the old saying, Mr. Graham—any port in a storm."

Picking up a blank, he wrote:

Confirm port screw fouled by cable and rudder jammed. Have many casualties. Location Yokohama outer harbor. Greatly appreciate any assistance. Signed, Applebye, *Oriental Monarch*.

"So, Mr. Graham, perhaps we will get our relief tomorrow so we can give some relief ourselves. All we have to worry about is earthquakes, tornadoes, typhoons, or even strong southerlies. I don't like where we are, but we will have to live with it overnight. I just hope our *Masai* friend can do what he says."

Sparks was back at his key, smoke swirling around his head as Sam patted him briefly on the shoulder and went back to his quarters.

Holden found the Hong Kong Suite empty when he and Osgood went back to it. There were no casualties waiting to be seen, and Hannah, Madelaine, and the children seemed to have gone out. Dr. Osgood, looking around the empty room, gave a deep sigh. "No patients. I can't believe it,

Doctor. I think this is a chance for me to catch up with a short nap, if you don't mind."

"You've earned it, Doctor," Holden smiled. "I don't know what I would have done without your help, and that of your colleagues. This is an entirely new experience."

"It is for all of us," Osgood answered. "I gather you did war duty. So did I. Some of that was very rough, but this is a completely unusual affair. I had to tend to a bad train accident once—something of the same feeling, but it was a minor thing compared to this. I hate to think what it must be like in the city, and probably in Tokyo."

"Beyond belief," Holden murmured. "I don't think our worries are over. We'll be getting new people aboard, I'm sure."

"Where are the ladies and the children?" Osgood asked. "They're such wonderful little tykes—I assume they have been orphaned."

"They must be getting some air. Yes. I gather they are orphaned. A problem for the consul, I'm afraid."

"Miss Clare is being so good with them."

"Yes," Holden agreed. "She struck me as very frail and out of it when I first saw her, but she has rallied around wonderfully. She and her companion have been a great help looking to the comfort of the casualties. And she is fine with the children. It must be hard, when they're so confused and lost. The little girl still talks of her mummy and daddy, but I'm afraid the boy knows exactly what's happened. He's doing his best to be brave. Miss Clare is doing everything she can to keep their spirits up."

"I have never seen her in a film, but I have heard she is quite famous."

"Yes. I have seen her once or twice, and she is lively and beautiful on the screen. It's too bad one can't hear her in a film. Her voice is so wonderfully soft and musical."

"Well, this is no film, but she's a heroine, I'd say. I'm off to my cot for a while." Osgood waved a hand as he went out.

Holden's thoughts went immediately to the vodka bottle in the cabinet, and he had a small struggle with himself. With all the heroism around them, should he still be weak and keep up his habit, his secret crutch? If Madelaine could swear off paregoric, he should be strong too—but he had a last-minute relapse, went to the cupboard, and took a quick shot. The beds nearby were an attractive magnet, and, shedding his jacket and kicking off his shoes, he quickly stretched out, dropping off almost immediately.

His next awareness was of someone standing over him, and he looked up to see Madelaine smiling down at him. As he struggled into consciousness, she leaned over and kissed him on the lips, then sat on the edge of the bed and ran her hand tenderly across his cheek.

"Do you mind my waking you?" she asked softly.

"I love it," he murmured. Waking up more, he asked, "Where are the children?"

"Hannah has them on deck, trying to play shuffleboard. It's a lovely day, and we seem to be out of the harbor, away from all those fires." She paused, still caressing him. "In case you're worried, I've locked the door. No one's in the sitting room now."

"Oh." His eyes met hers and held them.

"You said you wanted to sleep with a movie star under better circumstances."

"And this is it?"

"Isn't it?" She leaned over and kissed him with a sweet, demanding eagerness. "I've wanted you since the first moment you came to my cabin. You're so sweet and gentle, but you're strong too. Does this frighten you?"

He laughed softly. "Only that I'll wake up and find it's just a dream. A dream I've had since I first saw you."

"I was surprised to find you here, and I've been standing here for a while looking at you." She put a hand in his hair and ruffled it. "You look so sweet and handsome when you're asleep. It's a long time since I watched a man sleep."

"It's a long time since a woman watched me," he said.

"It made me want to make love." She started to unbutton his shirt slowly, smiling at him as he looked up at her with wide eyes. When the shirt was unbuttoned, she pulled it from his shoulders and dropped it to the floor, then came against his naked chest and they kissed fiercely. Her hands moved over his back, and he held her in a strong hug.

After a while, leaning back, she murmured. "Clothes are such a nuisance." She stood up, shedding hers, while he got out of his pants, then she threw herself down beside him, and he rose to cover her body, caressing and kissing her. Words stopped, with urgency growing, and the climax was strong and mutual.

At last he fell on his back beside her, kissing her neck softly and brushing his hand across her breasts with a light caress.

"God but you are wonderful," he murmured in her ear.

"We are wonderful," she whispered to him, and they lay quietly, catching their breath and gently running their hands over each other.

"It has been a long time for me," she said.

"And for me too."

"I have been only half living for so long; giving up. But being near you, watching you with people, wanting to help you, and wanting to touch you has brought me alive again. Do you understand?"

"Yes. I've been the same way. My marriage broke up almost two years ago, and I've been drifting. Have you been married?"

"Yes. When I was seventeen, to a sweet boy, but he couldn't take my being in movies. He got more and more restless and jealous, and we broke up after less than a year. Since then, it has been mostly work. Oh, I've had affairs—how could you help it in my business? But not really involved. Nothing to make me feel like this."

She rose up and kissed him, then lay back again.

"How about you? Your marriage?" she asked.

"I guess the word is incompatible. Lots of small things, and I had a long period of adjustment getting over my war experiences. I wasn't much of a person."

"The war must have been terrible."

"Yes." He fell silent. "Yes, it was."

They lay without talking for a while, and at last she sat up. "I'm afraid we must be sensible now. They'll be back here before long." She got up and went into the bathroom, and he heard water running. When she came out, she said, "Your turn, if you want to," and began to put her clothes on. He took a quick shower and came out to dress.

"You must be terribly tired," she said. "I should have let you sleep."

"Are you kidding?" he laughed. "I can take on every casualty in Japan now. I'm a tiger." He grabbed her and gave her a strong hug, kissing her with a great surge of affection. "And don't think this is the end. You will be seeing a lot of me."

"I would like that. I want to know you very well." She smiled at him.

"For a one-day acquaintance we're not doing badly."

They both laughed and he went to the door and opened it cautiously.

"No one here yet," he said. "Your timing was perfect, my lady. And I have to get back to work."

"I know. I know. It's very important. But you won't have to prescribe for me any more. You've cured me."

"Best cure I know," he laughed, kissing her quickly again and putting on his jacket. He went over to the examination table and began to straighten it up. He could see, across the passageway, that Wheeler still had refugees checking in with him.

"What do you think will happen with the children?"

Madelaine asked as she sat on the settee. "I'm terribly worried about them."

"I don't know. Wheeler will have to find out where they can go, I guess. They must have some relatives."

"I don't think they do," she answered. "They know that their grandparents are all dead, and they don't seem to know about any aunts or uncles. Evidently their parents were both only children. It seems strange, but I suppose it's possible."

"There will have to be some agency, or something," he said.

"Oh. How awful." She fell silent, frowning.

"If that Davidoff were any kind of a human being, he could do something for them, but I would hate to see that. He's a miserable man from what I saw of him."

"That wouldn't do. It just wouldn't do," she cried.

"I agree. We'll just have to see what ideas Wheeler has, I guess. But you're been so important to them now. They're lucky they found you." He paused. "Almost as lucky as I am," he said softly.

There was a knock at the passageway door, and two refugees who had been treated before asked to come in and have their dressings looked at.

"Yes. Come in," Holden told them. To Madelaine, he said, "Here we go again, but don't go too far. Stay where I can see you."

"I'm here where I can see you. And I will do anything I can to help." Their eyes held before he turned to attend to the patients.

Sam telephoned Wheeler in the Yokohama Suite and asked him to come to the bridge with information on the number of refugees aboard.

When Wheeler arrived, he found Sam on the wing of the bridge scanning the harbor with binoculars.

"Are we in a better situation now, Captain?" Wheeler asked. "I still don't know how you were able to maneuver out here under the circumstances."

"It has been difficult, I'll grant you that, Mr. Wheeler, and I'm by no means happy with where we are yet. This is an uneasy anchorage. We can't go much further forward on this heading without running aground, and I can't make the ship turn to starboard with only the starboard screw working, and no rudder."

"I gather the tug that came alongside was no help."

"No. They didn't know how to take a tow properly, but we'll have to find some way to bring her bow around. I understand from a British naval vessel at Yokosuka that they may be able to arrange for a dive team to come here tomorrow morning and attempt to free the jam. Meanwhile, I'm going to try kedging the bow around. I don't have much confidence that it will work. It's a soft bottom here."

"You'd rather be outside in Tokyo Bay?"

"Yes. Exactly. There are still some fires on both sides of the harbor, and the water is still covered with oil. I won't feel easy until we're away from the oil spills completely. More fires could come at any time. At least the breeze is calm now."

"You asked for the refugee figures, Captain."

"Ah, yes. I have to report them to Kobe. We also just got orders to remain here indefinitely as a relief station. I'd like to know myself just how many mouths we have to feed. It's lucky we were at the beginning of a voyage instead of the end, or we wouldn't be so well stocked."

"Well, by my latest count, we have 592 Europeans, 705 Japanese, and 604 Chinese and other Asiatics."

"Whew! What a shipload," Sam paused, doing mental arithmetic. "I make that about 1900 altogether. So with our own passengers and crew that's almost 3000 aboard. That's a real strain on our facilities and our people.

"Yes, Captain. Still, everyone is doing an amazing job. I'm impressed with both your crew and with the passengers."

"I just hope it won't all be lost by our being caught in this place. It's going to be an uneasy night if we can't kedge our head around."

"How about one of these vessels anchored near us acting as a tug. Would that work?"

"Most of them seem to be abandoned, and I'm afraid it would take a professional tug man to do it properly. Even the official tugboat did a poor job, as you saw. I'm sure her captain could not have been aboard."

"Just a thought."

"I would try it if we were more directly threatened by fires, but we'll cross our fingers that none comes up during the night. On another matter, Mr. Wheeler, I'm anxious to send any serious casualties to Kobe—people who need more attention than we can give here with our limited facilities and equipment. I've been told there are a few, and I gather we've had a death among the refugees. If you could give me an idea of how many cases there are, I will try to arrange something. I don't know what, yet, but I would like to."

"Yes sir. I will find out. Meanwhile, let's hope for a calm night and no fires."

"By all means, Mr. Wheeler. By all means." Sam sighed.

When Wheeler had gone and the radio message to Kobe had been sent to the wireless, Sam conferred with Perkins about running a kedge anchor out to starboard in an effort to bring the bow around with it. While Perkins was getting the motor lifeboat ready, Sam kept up his vigil around the harbor for any signs of danger, and his thoughts wandered back to the past, as they seemed to do at crises in his career. That old but very true cliche of how small coincidences and variations in time can have an enormous influence on a life, came home to him strongly.

The night when he had been on his way home to his

family's house in Hull, disgruntled but with no thoughts of a change in his life, and his future set with the family company, it had come to rain suddenly and hard. He had ducked into the pub to get out of the rain as much as to have an ale. And there had sat Jack Pearson, with his wild scheme of heading for gold in Canada. And when he had applied on a long shot for a job at C & O after giving up on the gold fields, it was just a matter of timing that the fourth mate of the old *Northland* had come down with appendicitis just before sailing time. The company had had no time to look for any other applicant, and he had gotten the job.

He had been asked to fill in as an escort for Alicia at a company banquet when the man who was supposed to take her was called out of town unexpectedly. As for Mikaela, she had been a last-minute addition to the captain's table on the voyage that brought her to Japan. That was because of a change of plans of the passenger who had been assigned. He couldn't imagine that he wouldn't have somehow gotten to know her, and the thought of never having known her made him shiver.

If this quake had been only fifteen or twenty minutes later, with the *Monarch* headed out of the inner harbor, the ship would have avoided all the incredible things that had happened to her over the past twenty-four hours. But then Mikaela would not have been rescued, and, if she had been up in her apartment, would certainly have been killed.

It was too much to contemplate, and he forced himself to stop the train of thought and concentrate on the present. Perkins had the lifeboat under the bow now, and the anchor was being carefully lowered into the boat. The biggest anchor was too heavy for the boat to handle; this was a smaller kedge, and Sam had no confidence that it would work. Still it had to be tried. He could only watch and wait as the boat ran slowly out at an angle to the starboard bow and the crew levered the kedge over the side. It went in with a great splash, and the small boat rocked crazily in reaction to the release from the load.

Now came the test. Sam watched anxiously as the windlass began to turn, waiting to see if the anchor cable would take tension. He had a surge of hope when it straightened out and went taut. Would it hold? Just when it seemed that it might, it suddenly slackened and the anchor dragged. The bow never moved at all. Sam ordered the anchor detail on the bow to try again and the long process of getting it back aboard and back in the boat continued for three attempts—but the harbor bottom was too soft, and the whole effort was a laborious failure.

PART

IV

PART

IV

CHIN CHING opened the door to Mikaela's cabin softly, bringing a tray of tea and biscuits. As he started to put it on the top of the dresser, Mikaela stirred, opened her eyes, and looked up at him blankly.

"Excuse me, Miss," he murmured. "I have hot tea and biscuits if you like. I think maybe you need. You want sleep more?" She started to answer in Swedish, then paused. "Oh, thank you," she said, still confused. "Yes. I am hungry. What has happened? Where are we?"

"We go out harbor to new anchorage outside. How you feel?"

"I can't tell yet. I feel very confused."

"You have shot from doctor. Make you sleep. Your leg hurt?"

"Yes. Yes. I guess it does."

"You have splints now. Doctors fix while you sleep."

"Oh my goodness. And I never knew!"

He poured some tea into a cup and offered her the plate of biscuits. She groped for one, dropping it, then finally picked it up and began to take small bites.

"You want tea?"

"Oh, yes please." She tried to struggle up and gave a small cry. "I'm not sure I can do it."

"I help," he said, and very gently raised her so that she was leaning against the pillow. He held the cup and saucer in front of her and steadied her hand when she took the cup and raised it to her mouth. She took small, weak sips, and some ran down her chin. He touched it with a napkin and waited until she had composed herself. Inching up higher, she was able to take the next sip more easily.

"My goodness," she sighed. "How long is it since I had anything to eat?"

"Is afternoon, Miss. Maybe whole day you no eat. This do you good."

"Oh, yes," she answered, concentrating on drinking for a while, then eating another biscuit.

"How is the captain?" She broke the long silence.

"Captain do good. He busy moving ship. Ask for you many times. I tell him you sleep, but he come now, I think maybe, now you awake."

"I don't want to bother him. I know what it must be like to be in charge of the ship. So many responsibilities."

"Big fire on water almost catch ship in harbor, but captain, he take ship to safe place just in time. Fire come, we all burn, but captain take ship to good place just in time."

"When I was coming out in the lifeboat, I heard people saying what a wonderful job he had done. They said something about his being made captain of the new company ship."

"Yes, Miss. He going to be captain of big new ship. Top job in company. People from company on board here so happy captain do well. They say how family proud of him, and company too."

"Is it official?"

"Yes, Miss. I think so."

"How do you know?"

"I show you. You wait." He slipped out the door while she sipped the tea and had another biscuit. He was back soon with a piece of paper that he pulled out from the sleeve of his jacket.

"You look," he said. "Here." He pointed to a place on the page. It was Alicia's letter to Sam. Chin Ching took the cup from Mikaela, and she slowly focused on the paragraph with Alicia's report on the board meeting.

"How did you get this?" she finally asked, after reading it twice. "It's a private letter." She handed it back to him.

"Captain leave on desk. I see when I clean desk."

"I'm afraid you shouldn't show it to me, but I do thank you. I know he has a very important job."

"Captain best ship captain in world. New ship belong him, because he top man. He my captain always, and I very happy he get new ship. You understand, Miss?"

"Yes, Chin Ching, I think I do. Thank you for showing me the letter. Put it back quickly. No one should know we have seen it."

"Yes, Miss. Yes, Miss. I do. I come back," he said as he again went out the door. He was back soon to help her with the cup, and she sipped her tea thoughtfully.

"How long have you been with the captain?" she asked.

"Maybe fifteen year now. I start with him on old ship when he make captain first time. I stay with him all through war when navy take over his ship. We take soldiers all over world. Many big convoys. Then we go to Scotland and bring this ship back to Vancouver. She German ship English win in war."

"Yes. I know. And she's a lovely ship."

"Next ship be bigger. Faster too."

She sighed and handed the empty cup to him. "Thank you so much. I do feel better now. I was so weak. I'm still weak." She gave a small helpless laugh and settled back against the pillow.

"Chin Ching. I have one more problem. I'm afraid I cannot go to the bathroom by myself."

"Ah yes, Miss. I help. You wait." He left the cabin and was soon back with a bedpan. "I get from doctor. He glad

✴ 163 ✴

you awake. He come to see you." He helped her with the bedpan, and she smiled weakly at him when she was finished.

"I'm sorry to be such a nuisance. You're very good to me, besides having saved my life. It's embarrassing to be so helpless. You're a very good nurse."

While he was taking the pan to the bathroom down the passageway, Holden came to the door, looked in for a moment, then entered. "Ah. You're awake. I hope you feel rested."

"Goodness. I slept for hours and hours. I've lost all track of time. Chin Ching says we're out in the bay now."

"Yes. We're in a better spot, but we still have trouble. More problems for the captain to get us out to Tokyo Bay."

"I understand he has done a marvelous job."

"Oh yes. He's pulled the ship out of some amazing scrapes. It's been a tremendous responsibility for him." He paused. "How are you feeling? Is the leg still painful?"

"Yes, it is, but I feel much better now that I'm clean and have had some sleep."

"Your break is a serious one, I fear, and it must be operated on in a proper hospital for the bone to be set correctly. We've done what we can here, for now. We will try to do something about the pain, and I hope we can get you to a hospital before too long. I see that the excellent Chin Ching is being a good nurse. Is the pain bad now? I can give you another shot."

"I'd rather not for a while. I think I can stand it. Please don't worry about me. And thank you for what you have done."

"I'll check back with you soon."

He left, and Chin Ching stood by the door.

"Captain come soon, Miss. I tell him you awake."

"Oh, thank you. I shouldn't take him from his duties."

"He come, I think." Chin Ching bowed and disappeared.

* * *

Madelaine stood by Holden as he worked on the casualties, helping him with new bandages, disposing of old ones. Occasionally their eyes met and they both felt a wonderful sense of sharing. She no longer had any make-up on, and her hair fell in loose strands over her forehead; he was struck by the natural sweetness of her looks—a gentle beauty quite removed from the movie star aura that she had presented at first. Her large, very blue eyes were perhaps her most noticeable feature, and there was a glow in them, a warmth, that lit her whole face.

Hannah and the children, each clutching one of her hands, came back to the suite, and Madelaine gave both of them a hug as they came to her.

"How is it on deck?" she asked. "Did you have fun?"

"We played shuffleboard," Peter said. "We weren't very good," he added, pouting.

"I beat Peter once," Susan said. Peter shrugged and bowed his head.

"How did it go?" Madelaine asked Hannah.

"It's a lovely warm day," Hannah said. "It seems so strange after yesterday to have everything so calm and peaceful, but you can see smoke and fires along the shore. There are so many refugees all over the decks it was a bit strange to be playing a game. They tried to do it right."

"Well I'm sure the air did them good. Shall we have some tea or something else to drink?" she asked the children. "Let's go in the bedroom. The doctor's busy here."

She put her hands on their shoulders, giving each a small hug, and smiled at Holden as she shepherded them through the door.

"I'll see what I can find," Hannah said as she left them.

"Well," Madelaine said. "I'm glad you could get on deck for a while. Did you ever play shuffleboard before?"

"No," Peter answered. "I remember the ship that brought us to Japan, but Susan doesn't. I didn't play shuffleboard. I

* 165 *

was too little, but I think Mummy and Daddy did. Daddy is—was very good at games."

He fell moodily silent, realizing what he had just said, and the awkward correction. Finally, very softly, he muttered "I forgot."

Madelaine, unable to say anything, hugged him tighter, and he suddenly looked up at her. "Will the ship go back to Yokohama? What are we going to do?"

She took a while to answer him, biting her lip. "No, dear. I don't think the ship will go back to Yokohama, because it's all wrecked. The houses are all knocked down. You can stay here on the ship with Hannah and me, and we'll take care of you. When things calm down and everyone's not busy, then we'll see about plans."

"I'll never see Marcia and Buffy again," Susan said sadly.

Madelaine looked at her questioningly and Peter said, "Those are her dolls. And I had my train set. And all our clothes."

The children sat on one bed and she sat on the other, facing them. A brief flash of memory of what had gone on there a few minutes before filled her with a strange sadness, and she was afraid, for a moment, that she might start to cry. Her eyes felt moist and her throat was too choked for her to speak. Then, getting control of herself, she began to talk to them.

"We'll have to see about more clothes when we get the chance. We can wash things when you're asleep until we can find some more. We can't make any real plans now, but maybe you can tell me some more about your relatives. I know you said that you don't have any grandparents living."

"Yes," Peter nodded. "We never knew them."

"Do you know about any aunts or uncles or cousins?"

Peter looked thoughtful, then answered hesitantly. "I don't know. I don't think so. Mummy and Daddy used to say things about our being the whole family we had. There was nobody in Yokohama, anyway."

"Did you get letters or birthday cards or Christmas presents?"

"Mummy gave me Marcia and Daddy gave me Buffy," Susan piped up.

"I don't remember any," Peter answered slowly. "Michiko, our nanny, she lives in Yokohama." He paused. "I mean, she did, I guess. She used to joke and say that she was our Japanese aunt."

Susan suddenly started to cry. "We won't see Michiko either?"

Madelaine moved over and took them in her arms, comforting her in silence.

"Hannah and I will be your American aunts," she finally said, smiling at them.

"We've never been to America," Peter said.

"Maybe you can come and visit me. I live in California. It's very nice. The weather is warm and sunny and there are beautiful beaches."

"We were going to the beach yesterday," Susan spoke up. "Mummy had our bathing costumes in a bag." She fell silent again.

"You're very nice to us." Peter looked up at Madelaine. "But you don't really know us, and we don't know you."

"Oh, but we do know each other now! We're friends," she cried.

"The man from the ship who brought us here he took us to Mr. David—uh, the man Daddy worked for, but I never liked him. And Daddy didn't either. I heard him tell Mummy that once. He was a mean man, but Daddy had a good job working for him. And he wouldn't take care of us anyway. He wouldn't let us in his cabin. I hope we don't have to go with him. I like you much better."

"Oh, no. You won't have to do that. He's too busy to

have anything to do with children, I think. No, you stay with Hannah and me and just for fun you can call us Aunt Hannah and Aunt Madelaine, and then it'll be a little like we're a family. Do you think that's a good idea?" She saw that Peter looked doubtful. "You have to call us something, don't you?"

"All right." He paused. "All right, Aunt Madelaine," he said brightly, and Susan giggled. She leaned over and kissed them both.

"There. We're like family now, and Hannah and I will try very hard to be good aunts. You know, I've never been an aunt before." She laughed. "I think this will be fun."

Perkins and the workboat crew came back alongside the ship from the long, futile attempt to kedge the bow around. He, the bosun, and the three seamen who had been working with them, were wet and streaked with mud. They were a dejected crew as they moored the boat to the boom. All of them were tired from the long night of work without sleep and all the tensions since the quake hit, and the failure of the anchor to take hold had made the fatigue even more acute. Perkins wondered whether they had failed in some way in what they had done, but he couldn't think of anything they could have done differently.

They had been too busy to study the condition of the ship, but now he looked up and saw the scratches and bare patches of steel where they had crashed along the French ship, and there were dents and scars all along the upper part of the hull from the collisions with the *Cape Fear* and the *Renaissance*. Along the waterline there were more scars and bare patches where the ship had plowed through the big raft of wreckage on the way out of the inner harbor, and smudges on the hull and superstructure from the fires on the Customs pier. The old girl's taken a beating, he thought. It was incredible what the ship had been through, and he was truly sorry that they had not been able to kedge the bow around and get her out of the trap she was still in.

At the memory of the fires, he had a flash of guilt over his behavior on the bow when they were getting the anchor in earlier this morning. He grunted in disgust. Why had he done that? He couldn't explain it to himself, and he was aware of the way the bosun had been regarding him ever since. He was a tough old hand with a background of Cape Horn sailing ships—a fine seaman and as strong as an ox. Perkins had been in awe of him. He realized that the old hand looked on him as a green newcomer, but the formalities had always been properly observed. Now he detected a brusqueness and a subtle lack of respect, and he wished there was some way he could take back the foolish panic that had sent him into the companionway hood. He could blame it on lack of sleep, but that was no help either. He simply was ashamed of himself and upset at the thought of the opinion the bosun must have of him. The man had stared him down with a cold eye once or twice as they were working, and now was ignoring him as much as possible.

While they were making the boat fast, he looked around the bay to see if there were any changes in the situation. It was a warm, calm day, and there was infinite irony in the bright sunlight shining down on a scene of such recent chaos. He scanned the shoreline, now a good distance away beyond the inner harbor. There were plumes of smoke rising in several locations. Evidently all the fires had not been put out, and there were still patches of oil on the water, even here in the outer harbor. There were many small coastal ships anchored near them, though quite a few had been making their way out during the day. The ones that remained were probably abandoned. The only course to open water, off the starboard bow, was fairly free of anchored craft. If only they could have pulled the bow around! Things would be so much easier and safer if they were finally outside in

Tokyo Bay. Somehow it almost seemed worse to be aware of the dangers that still lay all around them under this calm, sunny sky, than to have the very obvious perils of fires and typhoon winds directly assaulting them. Along with his feeling of guilt and remorse, he had a gnawing sense of dread, increased by the sight of the ship's scars and dents, and the awareness of the crippled rudder and starboard propeller.

With the boat secure, he started to head for the ladder to climb to the ship. The bosun, without so much as a backward glance, shouldered his way to the ladder ahead of him and climbed aboard—a breach in etiquette that Perkins recognized all too well.

Watching the frustrated anchor detail give up on the kedging, Sam felt a profound sense of disappointment for a moment. Would the troubles never end? Off his starboard bow in the blue distance, the open waters of Tokyo Bay beckoned tantalizingly, but here sat the *Monarch*, a helpless giant, waiting for some miracle to free her from the predicament she was still in, so near and yet so far from ultimate safety. Because safety seemed so near, the sense of peril was even greater, the edgy feeling of unease even more disturbing. His shoulders sagged, and the binoculars fell against his chest. He had been using them constantly to check the situation all around the harbor—the pillars of smoke on shore, the shining pools of oil on the water, and the rafts of wreckage and abandoned lighters and sampans. The immediate problem was to escape from the dangers of Yokohama Harbor, and then would come an indefinite period of stress acting as relief headquarters. He knew it had to be done, he knew that *Oriental Monarch* had to be it, and yet it put such an extra burden on the ship, the crew, and, of course, on him.

Through it all, he could never get Mikaela out of his

mind. There had to be some way to get her the attention she had to have, but he couldn't take her to safety on the ship in the foreseeable future. He would have to try to arrange some way perhaps with *Masai*, to get her and the other critical cases to the hospital in Kobe.

His mood of sodden despair was broken by Sparks, who came onto the bridge carrying a message, typed out this time.

"Wireless from *Masai*, Captain." He handed him the sheet. "Just received."

Frowning, Sam started to read.

Dangerous situation at naval base here. Several large ships lost to burning oil in bay. *Masai* safe. Loaded with severe casualties and departing for Kobe soonest. If you have critical medical cases have room for twelve and will send launch to pick up from you. Arriving there 1700. Advise if you wish comply. Dive team to effect your repairs promised for 1100 tomorrow.

Sam smiled inwardly as he read it. At least here was the solution for Mikaela, and the note about the dive team was a positive one. They would just have to get through the night safely before the ship could fend for herself again—if the dive team could take care of the jammed cable.

"That's helpful, Sparks. Very helpful. Reply that we will have twelve casualties ready for their launch at 1700, my signature."

He checked his watch—a little over two hours. Moving to the phone, he called the Hong Kong Suite and gave Holden the word about the twelve most serious casualties. "Is Mrs. Swenson awake?" he asked. "She should be one of the twelve, and we should let her know."

"Yes, Captain. I just talked to her a few minutes ago.

She is awake, and Chin Ching has given her some tea and biscuits."

"Can she be moved safely?"

"Yes. By stretcher. We'll be very careful, and I'll sedate her before she leaves."

Although it was a relief to know that help was on the way, Sam was filled with a feeling of sadness, a sense of loss, at the thought of Mikaela leaving. It was the best thing, the only thing, but he hated to think of it. At least she was awake now, and he would be able to see her for a while. As long as no emergency came up, he could spend these last minutes with her. When would he see her again? The awful devastation of the earthquake and its incredible destruction had torn his own world completely apart as surely as it had ripped the streets and buildings of Yokohama. What were his own troubles against those of thousands of people who had lost their lives and the millions more who were injured and homeless? But that made it no easier to face the multiple problems that crowded in on him now. If he could only take the launch with Mikaela—chuck the whole thing and stay with her till she was well—but he shook his head and grunted aloud, knowing the impossibility. The phrase in the wireless from the *Masai* was enough to remind him of the situation: "Several large ships lost to burning oil in the bay." Again came the awful image of flames surrounding the *Monarch*, and the knowledge that he could do nothing for the ship or the thousands aboard her should flames engulf her.

He would have to spend some time with Mikaela before the launch came, but he could not leave the bridge without relief. Robertshaw was either working with Wheeler or sleeping. Let him sleep. The man had been very little help. Barclay would have to be it, and he sent the bridge messenger to his cabin. Barclay soon appeared, rubbing his eyes and straightening his uniform.

"You sent for me, Captain?"

"Yes, Mr. Barclay. Sorry to wake you, but I want some time to myself, if you will take over the bridge. All seems quiet for the moment. There is oil about and there are some fires along the shore, but nothing is threatening us now. Call me if there is any change of any sort. I will be in the pilot's cabin."

Barclay's eyes widened slightly at this information, but he made no comment other than to say "I relieve you sir."

Chin Ching was helping Mikaela to sit up against the pillows when Sam arrived at the cabin door. She was pale, and there were bruises on her forehead and cheek, but she had managed to smooth her hair and it spread in a golden cloud across the pillow, framing her face. She still wore the man's bathrobe Chin Ching had found for her. When she saw him, her eyes shone with delight and she smiled a soft, sad smile, holding out her hand to him. Chin Ching bowed and silently backed out the door, and Sam came to her and took her hand in both of his. He held it tightly, and neither spoke for a long moment.

"I'm so glad you came," she almost whispered, her voice breaking. "But should you? There is so much to do for the ship. I know you have had many, many troubles."

"Right now things are calm," he answered. "I had to come when I heard you were awake. How do you feel? Are you still in pain?"

"Yes, my leg hurts, but I feel much better now that I have had some sleep and some tea. And I am clean. Chin Ching has been a very good nurse."

"I'm glad." He moved his hand toward the bruises, but not to touch them. "You had such a time. So terrible."

"But I was saved."

"Yes, thank God." He bowed his head. "The doctor explained about your leg? That you need an operation?"

"Yes. He told me I would have to go to a regular hospital."

"That is true, and we have arranged for it. There is a ship leaving for Kobe in two hours."

She clutched at his hand and gave a small cry. "Oh. Leave here?"

"Yes. It's the best thing. If you aren't operated on soon, the results could be very serious." He paused, as she bit her lip and her eyes shone with tears. "It is the best thing. The only thing. The ship will be here for at least a week on relief duty, and we can't take care of you properly. You can't afford to put it off, my dear."

She leaned back against the pillow with a sigh, and the folds of the bathrobe fell open, showing the soft curves of her breasts. It was a reminder to him, a poignant memory of the love they had made, of the joy and passion they had shared, of the wondrous discovery for him, at his age, of just what such lovemaking could mean. It had come so late to him, which had made it all the more important. He thought back to the night before last, which seemed centuries ago now, and a surge of emotion filled him, tightening his throat and bringing tears to his eyes.

"I want to be with you," she murmured.

"And I want to be with you. We will be in Kobe within the week. You should be much better by then, with the operation all done. We can celebrate."

"Oh. I know it's best. And you will be so busy it is selfish of me to think we can spend any time together." She smiled at him. "But I want to make love to you right now."

His chuckle turned into a half-sob. "I too, I too. And wouldn't that be something? Your leg would probably stay broken forever."

"Ah, no. Not with my tender lover." She smiled again. "At least we can imagine, can't we?"

"It takes an earthquake to keep us apart."

They fell silent, her hand in his again, and he leaned forward and brushed his lips against the swell of her breast, the gentlest of touches. He looked up at her, smiled, and then did the same to her other breast and lifted his head again, sitting back.

"That, my dear, is about it for lovemaking now. But let it be a reminder of what our lovemaking has been, and what it will be."

She put her hand to his cheek and smiled softly, sighing.

"It has been so good," she said. After a silence, she changed her tone. "I understand you are to have a new big ship to command. That is wonderful news."

"Where did you hear that?"

"I heard Mr. Graham from your company say so when we were coming out in the lifeboat."

"Well I guess it's so, but it's not very much on my mind at the moment. Right now I am only thinking of you, but there are so many other things that have to be done here. The ship is still in a very dangerous spot until we can get out of this harbor to open water. We can't turn the ship to head out that way until someone helps us turn, or divers fix our propeller and rudder. Maybe you're lucky to be going to Kobe. If a fire catches us here, a broken ankle would be the least of your worries."

"Oh, don't say that," she cried. "I will worry about you, but you are such a good captain I know it will not happen."

"Would it were true," he sighed. "Let's hope it won't, because I want to come see you when we get to Kobe."

"How will you know where I am?"

"I'll find out, don't you worry."

She smiled and picked up his hand and kissed it. "I keep thinking how lucky it was that someone got sick so that I ended up at the captain's table. We might never have met."

"I would have found you. We were fated to meet."

"A lovely fate." They fell silent again, with a long look into each other's eyes.

"Why will you come to Kobe? Won't you go straight to Vancouver?" she asked.

"We will have to get more food and fuel before we can cross the Pacific, especially if we stay here a week. We are feeding about 3000 people right now, very simply, but we can't keep that up for more than a week, and there won't be any supplies here. When, if ever, I don't know." He shook his head.

"What ship am I going on?"

"A British destroyer, *Masai*. She was at Yokosuka on a courtesy visit. We've been in touch with her by wireless. She is taking a load of casualties to Kobe and told us she had room for twelve from here. She is sending a launch..." he looked at his watch "...in a bit over an hour. The doctor wants to see you and get you ready for the trip, but we can still have some time together—a little while longer."

"Aren't you needed on the bridge? I worry that I am keeping you from your duties."

"Ah, yes. We have talked about duty, haven't we? You remember what you said about it?"

"Something like God damn it," she smiled. "But I was only joking."

"Partly, perhaps. Partly."

Suddenly she gave a small cry and clutched his hand again. "Oh, I don't want to leave you. I love you and I want to be with you."

"I love you," he said simply. "And how I wish that you and I could be off together somewhere by ourselves. Maybe someday we can. Maybe when life is a little less complicated than it is now, even without earthquakes. And someday," he chuckled, "airships will carry all the passengers and I won't have a job. I won't have to worry about *duty* any more. It's just a dream."

"It's a lovely dream. I have it too. We would be in a cottage by the sea, and we would have long, long days with nothing to do but to be together. Or maybe it should be in the mountains, not by the sea. Perhaps the sea will make you want to go on it. Once a sailor..."

He gave a short laugh. "Wherever I could be with you would be all right with me. By the sea, in the mountains, in a big city where we could go to restaurants and the theater..."

"And you have never been to Sweden. I could show you my lovely Sweden."

"I wouldn't bother you with Hull," he chuckled.

She hesitated, then suddenly spoke faster. "Would we have children? Would you like that?"

He fell silent and gave her a long look, then spoke very seriously. "Yes, I would like that. I would like it very much. I have always been sorry that I have never had children." He stopped and shook his head. "But we are getting a bit ahead of ourselves, my dear. Ahead of ourselves with beautiful thoughts, perhaps dreams—who knows? But we can't let them die, and we must get your leg fixed or I'll be pushing you around in a wheelchair in our dreams."

"No, Sam, no." She was serious again. "You are right. I must leave you and go to the hospital—and the pain in my leg tells me you are right, too."

"Yes. Before we turn into blubbering fools we must get you properly set for your boat ride. No more dreams for a while. We must just be practical." He straightened up and shook himself.

"Aye, aye, sir." She smiled at him through beginning tears.

"But don't lose the dreams. You will always be in mine." He stood, held her hand strongly, then leaned over and kissed her long and tenderly on the lips. "*Tak* for love."

✳ 177 ✳

"*Tak* for love," she answered, as he turned quickly and went out the door.

Madelaine settled the children for a nap, closed the bedroom door softly, and came out to the sitting room. There were no patients at the moment, and Holden was slumped on the settee, his eyes closed. He opened them and smiled at her as he heard her come close, and she brushed her lips across his before sitting next to him.

"You do the nicest things," he murmured.

"No one to work on now?" she asked.

"It's gone quiet. About time. I've been down around the decks and public rooms seeing if anyone was there who needed help. What a scene. What a mess. I once saw a railroad station in India during a flood evacuation, and our public rooms look just like that now. The aroma is a bit stiff too, but no one is complaining. Most of them have been attended to by now, so I didn't find much to do."

"You must be tired."

"Only routine. You set me up for the day, lady."

She gave a low laugh and kissed him again. This time he responded, finally settling back again. "Where are the children?" he asked.

"They're napping. I just tucked them in."

"Quite the little mother."

"I am now Aunt Madelaine. They were having a hard time knowing what to call me." She paused. "I'm really quite worried about them. As far as I know they have no other family; nowhere to go, and of course they just have the clothes they're wearing. They started talking about their toys and their nanny, and I don't know what to tell them."

"Yes. I can see. It is a problem."

"You mentioned there might be an agency—for orphans, I suppose, and that seems so awful, so cold blooded. They're sad and frightened enough as it is now."

"Well they can certainly stay with you for a few days while the ship's in this emergency. You've been a godsend."

"I'd love to keep them with me."

"You mean permanently?"

"Well, yes. I guess so. But I don't know how something like that could be arranged."

"Are you really ready for that serious a step?"

"I—I think so. I'd like to think so. Seeing all the tragedy there has been around us has made me feel very vain and selfish the way I've been living." She paused and smiled at him. "And you gave me a lovely cure, too."

"I think we cured each other. I can't tell you how much it has meant to me to have you here and to be doing things with you side by side."

"I'm so glad. We'll be together a lot now, I think, if the ship stays here as a relief station. The rest of the world seems so far, far away—almost non-existent."

"By the time we get to Vancouver, if we ever do, we'll be lifelong friends. And maybe we'll have a chance for some more curative sessions."

"I'd love to continue the cure." She moved closer to him and put her head on his shoulder. They sat quietly for a few minutes, his arm around her. There were sounds of people outside in the passageway, and someone knocked at the door. Slowly he stood up after giving her a last quick hug. "Back to work, I guess. Why don't you talk to Wheeler, the vice consul chap across the way. He might have some suggestions on the problem with the children."

He opened the door and let in two people who asked to see the doctor.

"Good idea. I will," Madelaine said, standing up and heading across to the Yokohama Suite.

Wheeler was seated behind his temporary desk, with only one person standing in front of it talking to him. When the man left, Madelaine came forward.

"Mr. Wheeler? May I ask your advice on something?"

"Yes, Miss Clare. Of course. How may I help?" He stood up and offered her a chair next to the desk.

"It's about the children."

"The Bridgemans?"

"Yes. You know that their parents were killed on the pier?"

"Yes. I was a good friend of the Bridgemans. It's very sad."

"As far as I know, they don't seem to have any relatives at all. Do you know of any?"

"Now that you mention it, I don't. I know that all the grandparents are dead, and I believe both Bridgemans were only children. They never mentioned any brothers or sisters."

"It seems very unusual, but that's what the children say, too. I've asked them if they got any Christmas or birthday presents from aunts or uncles, and they didn't remember any. Of course they're almost in a state of shock."

"I agree. It's most unusual, but probably true."

"Doctor Holden mentioned that you might know of an agency that would handle such cases."

"Offhand, I don't. But I can find out when things settle down a bit. Naturally, I don't have my usual sources of information here."

"Oh, it's so difficult, and an adoption agency for orphans sounds so impersonal, so...well, almost cruel."

"Of course there's nothing that can be done for some time," Wheeler said. "You have been so kind to take care of them, and I hope it hasn't been too much trouble for you. Can you keep them with you for a while?"

"Oh, yes. And what I would really like to do is keep them permanently if there is any way that's possible. I know it's unusual, but I've made up my mind. They're such dear, sweet children, and I would hate to see them turned over to some impersonal agency. They've had enough of a shock already, but they seem comfortable with Hannah and me. Do you think that's possible?"

Wheeler showed his surprise and took a minute to answer. "Well, I'm sure that it's possible. If they stay aboard the ship as long as you are aboard, I would think some temporary custody could be arranged, and then the question of permanent adoption could be gone into."

"Oh, that would be wonderful. I'd be so happy."

"I'm sure it's the best thing," he smiled at her. "And everyone is most grateful to you. Not many people in your position would be so helpful."

"Oh, thank you so much. We'll take very good care of them and finances are no problem. I have saved money. I'm most grateful." She paused. "Do you suppose there are some passengers with children who might have some extra clothes? All they have is the clothes they're standing in, and I would like to get them a change so we can keep them clean."

"Yes. I believe there are a few children among the passengers. I'll see what I can arrange."

"Oh, that would be marvelous. Thank you very much." She went back across to the Hong Kong Suite, and her eyes were glowing with pleasure as she smiled at Holden.

"I think it's going to work out," she told him. "Mr. Wheeler was very helpful and understanding."

"Great. I'm happy for you, and we'll all help. I've got to go up to the bridge for a moment. The captain wants me to tend to the injured woman his steward rescued. She's being transferred to the hospital in Kôbe because she needs an emergency operation on her leg. Hold the fort until I come back."

He gave her hand a squeeze and went out.

Barclay continued his bridge watch, keeping binoculars on the areas of fire on the shore and checking the other vessels in the harbor. There were fewer than there had been in the morning, when *Monarch* had made her tortuous way out of the inner harbor. Everything seemed secure, but he knew of the captain's anxiety. It was a gnawing worry at the back of his mind, and he wondered whether the port screw was permanently damaged or could be freed. The new-fangled German drive mechanism might have been a life saver with its flexibility under all the shocks the ship had suffered.

As he stood at the bridge rail and focused the binoculars on the inner harbor, watching an increased burst of smoke and flame at the eastern end of the shoreline, Robertshaw came out on the bridge.

"Any developments, Mr. Barclay?"

"Just watching that fire on the shore, Just flared up; only smoke before."

"Where is the captain?"

"Resting."

"Oh. I stopped by his quarters and he's not there."

"I believe he's in the pilot's cabin."

"With that woman?"

"He didn't say. I assume so."

"I understand from the doctors that we are to evacuate twelve casualties via a launch from the *Masai*, and she is one of them."

"I have not been told."

"Do you think she should be included? We—we have other casualties, other—" he stammered and stopped. "She should not be here anyway. The captain has—he is putting his own needs ahead of the ship's. This is very un—very irregular, very—" he passed a hand over his eyes and grasped the rail, his breath coming in short gasps.

Barclay stared at him. God, this bastard's on the edge. It's gotten to him. Looking to blame the captain. Thank God he's not in command. "As I said. I haven't been told."

Robertshaw took a deep breath, controlling himself. "It's very irregular. I'm not sure Mr. Wheeler will approve."

"If the captain orders it, it will be approved," Barclay said gruffly. His eyes leveled at Robertshaw and held in a long, glinting stare.

Robertshaw's eyes dropped under the stare after a moment, and he turned on his heel and left the bridge. Barclay glared at his back, then went back to scanning the shoreline until he was aware that Simms had come out on the bridge. He was still in stained, disheveled clothes and had a stubble of beard on his bruised face.

"Ah there, Simms," he greeted him. "Recovering from your ordeal? You look as though you've been through one."

"You can say that," Simms answered. "I think I'll live," he added sardonically.

"Anything I can do for you?"

"I was just interested in the vessels around us. I've fueled so many of them, you know, and I wondered how they have made out. The captain invited me to come up here any time."

"Yes. That's all right. You're welcome here. Here, have a look." He handed over the binoculars, and Simms began scanning around the harbor.

"There's the *Iris*," he said. "One of our yard tankers. I mean one of *their* tankers, now," he corrected himself with a sour laugh. "She seems to be abandoned. No one on board."

"Yes. I heard you'd had a shake-up," Barclay said.

"A shake-up and then an earthquake. Two big shake-ups."

"I'm sorry."

"So am I. So am I." Simms continued using the binoculars, occasionally commenting on a ship he recognized, then handed them back to Barclay. "Well, some of them made it, I see, but I'm afraid a lot were lost."

"Are you staying aboard, or do you plan to go back ashore?"

"I'm not sure. I decided to stay when I felt the after-shocks last night on that water detail. I know my flat is gone, but I guess I'll have to make up my mind. I don't know where to start over."

"That's a tough one. I feel for you. Did you have a family?"

"No, I'm a bachelor. At least I was spared that."

"Small comfort." Barclay fell silent and took up his scanning again.

"Keep a good eye on those fires, Barclay," Simms said. "There's a lot of oil about, and it won't take much to set it off again. I hope the captain can get us out of here soon."

"We all do, Simms. We all do," Barclay said as Simms walked away.

Holden found Mikaela writing on a pad when he came to the pilot's cabin. She was concentrating on her writing so thoroughly that she didn't see him at first, then looked up with a small cry of welcome.

"Oh, Doctor. I didn't hear you. Excuse me."

"Quite all right. And how are you feeling now?"

"It's painful. The captain tells me I am to leave the ship and have an operation so the break is properly set."

"Yes. That's so. As we said, we can't do it here with the limited facilities, and it's very necessary to avoid permanent damage. I'm sure you understand."

"I guess so, but I'm frightened. I hate to leave the ship."

"Of course."

"I'm writing a letter for the captain, but I don't want him to get it until I have left for Kobe. Will you hold it and give it to him later on, after the destroyer has left?"

"Why yes. I'd be glad to."

She gave him a direct, searching look, not knowing what to say for a moment, then decided to speak. "Doctor, you must know that it is the captain's child I am carrying. I hesitated to say so, but I want you to know."

"Yes. I would have assumed so, reading between the lines, so to speak."

"I don't want him to know about it. He has too much on his mind, too many responsibilities to the ship, to his family, to his company."

"Don't you think he would want to know?"

"Oh, yes. I know he would if everything were all right, but this is such a bad time."

"You're not going to tell him in the letter?"

"No. I am just saying goodbye. I want to go home to Sweden, where I have family and friends to help me. My leg will probably take a long time to be right, and I want to have the baby there. I am sure I can find a Swedish ship to book my passage home when I am out of the hospital. It is the best way."

"You're very brave. It will not be easy."

"I don't feel brave. I feel lonely, but it is the best thing for me to do."

"Perhaps you are depriving the captain of something he would like to know. Is he in love with you?"

"I believe so, and I love him. He is a fine man, but there is no room in his life now for something like this. Maybe someday I will let him know. I hope it is a son, a son just like his father." She choked back a sob and her eyes shone with tears.

"I hope it is the right thing." He looked at her searchingly. "Not an easy decision, I know that, and again, I admire you for your bravery. How will you manage? Money, clothes, credentials, all those things?"

"There is a Swedish consulate in Kobe. They will help me."

"Yes, that's right." He reached out and took her pulse, assuming a professional manner. "Now we must get you ready for the trip to Kobe. The launch will be here in a few minutes. I want to sedate you for the pain, but it would be better if you remain conscious, I think."

"Oh, yes. I want to be."

"I'll give you a milder sedative and hope that it does help some with the pain. And I've brought you a nightgown from Miss Madelaine Clare, the movie actress. She has been helping with the casualties, and her suite is a medical station. She's been most helpful."

"Oh, thank you." She smiled weakly. "I don't feel very well dressed in this robe."

"Keep that for warmth, too. Here. I'll help you change."

She shrugged out of the robe and put the gown over her head, then got back into the robe, which he held for her.

"Now for the shot," he said, and he gave it to her quickly and easily. "That should help."

"Would you wait a moment while I finish the letter?"

"Oh, yes. I'll arrange for a stretcher and be right back."

Frowning and biting her lip, with her hair hanging down over her face, she leaned over the pad and slowly finished the note, taking great care with each word. She read it over twice, touched it to her lips with a sigh, and put it in the envelope Chin Ching had given her with the pad and pen. Holden came back in, and she handed it to him.

"Here it is, Doctor. And remember—only after I have gone."

Sam joined Barclay on the bridge as the afternoon sun slanted in over the peaceful waters of the harbor. The sky was a clear, pale blue, and the gentlest of breezes sent small catspaws across the water where there were no patches of oil.

"Anything to report, Mr. Barclay?"

"Nothing special, Captain, except that one fire along

the inner shore. It seems to have flared up some, but it hasn't advanced this way at all."

"Good. May it stay that way. We're expecting a launch from H.M.S. *Masai* momentarily to take some of our worst casualties off. The doctors are supervising that down at the starboard gangway. Perhaps you should go down there to make sure everything goes properly. It'll be a ticklish business to lower the stretchers into the launch."

"I think I see the launch now, sir." Barclay pointed off to starboard.

"Ah, yes," Sam agreed. "I think you're right."

"Ah, Captain..." Barclay hesitated. "Just so you'd know, Mr. Robertshaw was up here looking for you a while ago."

"Oh." Sam looked at him for a moment. "Did he say what he wanted?"

"Had some idea about the casualties, sir. He thought Mr. Wheeler might not approve of the lady who was in the pilot's cabin being one of the twelve."

Sam looked at him stonily in a long silence. "He did, eh?"

"That's right, sir. I told him I believed it was your orders."

"It certainly is. You can be sure of that." Sam's face flushed and his eyes shone for a moment. "When you go down there, make sure that she is aboard, Mr. Barclay. My orders are not to be countermanded. If there is trouble, let me know."

"Aye, sir. Understood. That I will." Barclay hurried off the bridge.

Sam watched the *Masai*'s launch pull alongside, the chuffing of its exhaust slowing and quieting as it came to a stop. Every instinct made him want to be down there for a last glimpse of Mikaela, but he knew it would be wrong, and he stood quietly at the rail, looking down. Two of the patients could walk down the ladder with help, but the rest were stretcher cases. It was a long process to put the casualties aboard, as the stretchers had to be lowered by hoist, one by one, slowly and carefully. He kept the binoculars on the scene, and finally it was Mikaela's turn. She was lying quietly, but he could tell that her eyes were open. He thought she was looking at the bridge, and he raised his free hand in a slow gesture. Had she seen it? He wasn't sure, until, just before her stretcher was lowered down to the cockpit of the launch, her hand lifted from the stretcher and waved once. Then she was gone, hidden by the canopy of the launch. He slowly lowered the binoculars.

With the last of the twelve aboard, the launch's engine rumbled to life, and she pulled away from the ship's side, turning in a wide arc, and straightened out on a course out of the harbor and down the bay to Yokosuka. Sam watched her diminish slowly to a small dot and then disappear around the eastern point of the harbor. He kept his eyes there until even the faint path of the launch's wake had faded into the surface of the water, which gleamed quietly in the late afternoon light.

With a deep sigh, he took up his vigil with the binoculars again, watching especially the flare-up in the inner harbor that Barclay had pointed out. If the wind stayed calm, it was nothing to worry about. The sun, lowering redly off the port bow, sent a shimmering path across the harbor that reminded him of the surface fires of the day before and the morning. He shuddered at the memory.

Barclay came back to the bridge and reported in. "All secure, sir. No problems."

"Was Mr. Robertshaw there?"

"No, sir, but Mr. Wheeler was, and I asked him on the side if there was any hitch. He said no, that everything was set according to plan. She's aboard the launch now."

"Yes. I could see. Did she seem all right?"

"She was very quiet, but she did make a show of thanking Chin Ching. He should be back here soon."

"Thank you. I hope all goes well. She had a compound break that needed a complicated operation, or there was danger of an infection. The doctors couldn't handle it here."

"I understand."

"Well, I must go to my quarters for a bit. Will you stand by until 1800? I think Perkins is due then."

"Aye, sir. That I will."

"Call me, of course," Sam said as he went in to his quarters.

He had been lying down, resting his eyes and trying to take a short nap, but unable to still the gloomy thoughts of Mikaela's leaving and the still perilous position of the ship, when there was a hard rapping on his sitting room door.

"Yes. What is it?" He struggled up, rubbing his eyes.

"Robertshaw here, Captain."

"What now?" Sam groaned as he went to the door and opened it. Robertshaw, Graham, and two seamen wearing sidearms stood in the passageway. Shocked, Sam stared at them quietly, puzzled and annoyed.

"Yes?"

"We must have words with you, Captain." Robertshaw's face was drawn and taut. "Please let us come in."

"What is this about?" Sam asked gruffly. He stepped back, and Robertshaw and Graham came in, leaving the two men at the door. They were from the ship's security detail— Robertshaw's responsibility. Graham looked extremely uneasy, a worried frown on his face. When they were both inside, Robertshaw drew himself up stiffly, took a deep breath, and spoke loudly.

"Captain Applebye, representing the Canada & Orient Steamship Company, and on special orders of the Board of Directors..." he waved a piece of paper, "...and on the authority of the company's senior representative in this area, Mr. Graham, I am placing you under arrest in the matter of the murder of Sergei Davidoff. You are to remain in your quarters, which will be under armed guard, while I conduct an investigation."

Without answering, Sam turned his gaze on Graham with a look of steely scorn. Graham flushed and dropped his eyes, moving uneasily, then finally spoke, stammering. "It— it seems in order, Captain Applebye. Mr. Robertshaw has discovered some very unusual circumstances, and I'm afraid that we must have an explanation. He also has a special letter of authorization."

Sam continued to stare at them in silence, and Robertshaw broke in. "A murder has been committed and concealed under very suspicious circumstances, and since you were known to be the last person to speak to Mr. Davidoff, we declare that you are no longer fit to command this vessel."

"Have you heard of the word mutiny, Mr. Robertshaw?" Sam glared straight at him. "That's what you are doing now."

"I am acting under the authority of Mr. Graham, sir. This is a legitimate action, as you have committed a severe breach of your trust as commanding officer and a representative of the company."

"And if I walk out that door to the bridge are those men going to shoot me?"

"They have orders that you are to remain in your quarters."

"Well I won't put them to the test, because this can be cleared up very easily. Send for Mr. Stratford and Chin Ching. I'm not going to say another word until they are here."

"I'll see to it," Graham said, and he turned and slid out the door rapidly. Sam continued to stand without moving, staring at Robertshaw, the blue of his eyes glinting, his face a severe, lined mask. Robertshaw became more and more agitated, looking over his shoulder at the guards, dropping his eyes under Sam's gaze, and flicking the paper in his hand.

"I found him in the refrigerator when another casualty who was in there had to be identified, and there was that woman who..."

"Hold it, Mr. Robertshaw. Not now." Sam's voice was low and gruff.

They faced each other in uneasy silence until Chin Ching appeared outside. He looked in surprise at the armed men and Robertshaw, then turned to the captain.

"You send for me, Captain?"

"Yes, Chin Ching. Wait until Mr. Stratford gets here. These men have some questions they want to ask."

"Yes, Captain." Chin Ching could barely be heard. He stood aside quietly eyes lowered. Finally Graham and Stratford arrived and shouldered their way in.

"What is it, Captain?" Stratford asked, his face a picture of worry.

"Did I murder Mr. Davidoff?" Sam asked, before anyone else could speak.

"Murder!"

"Mr. Robertshaw and Mr. Graham are placing me under quarters arrest because of the strange circumstances of Mr. Davidoff's death, which Mr. Robertshaw has discovered."

"Good heavens!" Stratford looked at Graham and Robertshaw. "You both must be out of your minds. Captain Applebye is in command of this ship, and there is no reason to relieve him. Are you mad, Mr. Graham?" Stratford turned toward him.

"I—I—Robertshaw thought—it seemed—"

Stratford interrupted him. "The Captain and I went to Mr. Davidoff's suite to tell him we were commandeering it for a medical station, as he had refused to cooperate with us, and we found him lying on the floor, dead, with a bullet wound in his chest. It was at the height of the danger, with the ship alongside the burning pier. We both agreed there was no time to do anything about it then, so we had the body removed. Chin Ching and I took it down to the refrigerator room. Chin Ching can attest to that." He turned to look at Chin Ching, who nodded silently.

Robertshaw spoke rapidly, his voice high and breaking. "Why did you conceal it? This is very suspicious."

Stratford started to answer, but Sam interrupted. "Mr. Stratford has already told you. We had more important things to attend to, or the ship would have caught fire and none of us would have been worrying about Mr. Davidoff. We would be as dead as he was."

"But the authorities—" Graham started to say.

"What authorities, Mr. Graham?" Sam answered. "We had no contact with shore and no shore to deal with by that time. I am the authority, and it was my decision, agreed to by Mr. Stratford, that any investigation into Mr. Davidoff's death would have to be deferred until the ship was safe. I don't like having a murderer aboard any more than you or anyone else, but there was no other decision to make at the time."

"Why didn't you tell someone?" Robertshaw asked, shakily.

"What good would that have done? Mr. Stratford knew. Chin Ching knew. If anything happened to me, one of them could say what happened. And if you can picture conducting an investigation with 3,000 people on board, you're a better lawyer than I am. Nobody could have done anything for the time being. Now can we stop this nonsense, Mr. Graham? If we don't have a solution by the time we get to Kobe, it will be reported. Meanwhile, if we don't get the ship out of this harbor, there'll be a much bigger investigation, and a lot more corpses. Are you going to stop me from seeing to the welfare of my ship?"

"I'm sorry, Captain." Graham answered quickly, "I see your point. I didn't understand."

"Thank you. I will not charge Mr. Robertshaw with mutiny if he agrees to remain in his cabin until further notice. And I won't put an armed guard on him. Mr. Barclay can assume his duties. Am I making myself clear? Is this farce over with?"

Robertshaw collapsed on a chair sobbing, his head in his hands, and Graham spoke to him quietly. "We made a mistake, Mr. Robertshaw. The captain is right." He put a hand on Robertshaw's elbow and urged him up. Without another word, with his hands over his face, Robertshaw let Graham lead him out of the cabin leaving the letter behind. The two armed seamen looked confused, as Sam spoke to them. "You men did your duty, but the orders were wrong. Turn your arms in to Mr. Stratford and go about your regular duties."

They quickly stripped the gun belts and handed them to Stratford, then fled down the passageway. Stratford looked at the guns in his hands in surprise, and shrugged his shoulders.

Sam looked at him quizzically, a small grin on his face. "Do you suppose they would have taken a shot at me if I walked out of here?"

Stratford's mouth fell open, and he finally gasped, "What a thought, Captain, what a thought!"

"Thank God that's over," Sam sighed. "I was just trying to catch a nap." He passed a hand over his forehead. "Robertshaw has been out to get me ever since he came aboard, maybe on someone's orders—I don't know. Never did like him myself, and he has shown his true colors when things got tough, hasn't he? A nasty chap." He paused, gathering himself. "But I bloody well would like to know who the murderer is. It's not a nice thought to have him running loose on board, whoever he is. Well. It'll have to wait—and may Davidoff freeze in hell, as well as in our morgue," he muttered *sotto voce.*

"Thank you for your help, both of you. I'm glad I had witnesses. Chin Ching, I'm ready for supper now that the mutiny's over."

Chin Ching gave the smallest of smiles, bowed and went out.

"On to other things, eh Stratford?" Sam smiled at him as the purser started out. "And thank you again. Now all we have to do is save the ship."

He stood for a moment gazing around the cabin in bemused disbelief, then shook himself. Robertshaw, that miserable bastard, he thought, and picked up the letter that had been left behind on the desk.

It was marked Confidential and addressed to Robertshaw.

You are hereby authorized to represent the Canadian & Orient Company in checking on the performance of duty by Capt. Samuel Applebye as pertaining to his eligibility for promotion to Senior Captain of the Company and prospective captain of the new flagship. Of greater interest than his nautical competence, which is well known, is his personal behavior, and any involvement in activities, including extra-marital affairs, that could affect the Company's reputation. I have received unconfirmed rumors in regard to this matter. Because of obvious reasons, this has not come up for discussion at our Board meetings, and I am trusting your tact and judgement to keep this a completely confidential matter between you and the undersigned.

It was signed by the Chairman of the Board.

Sam sat unmoving, staring down at the letter, until Chin Ching appeared with supper on a tray. Shaking himself and slowly coming out of his concentration, he thanked Chin Ching absently and began to pick at his food.

He was still eating mechanically, staring off into space, with the letter crumpled in one hand, when there was a rap on the door and Holden asked to come in.

"Yes, doctor." Sam braced himself, threw the letter in the waste basket and faced Holden. "Casualties safely away, eh? No hitches?"

"That's right sir. All went well. I hope they can be helped in Kobe. Some of them were quite serious, and we've had two more die."

"Is that why Robertshaw went in the morgue?"

"What's that, sir?"

"Oh, excuse me," Sam shook his head. "I'm ahead of myself—thinking of other things. We've just had a little fuss and flare-up, and I think you had better know about it, since I assume you will have occasion to go into the morgue sometime."

"What is that, sir?"

"There's a body in there, and it's not an earthquake victim. It's that Davidoff. I think you saw him when he came aboard—he wouldn't take those children in."

"Yes, I remember. What happened?"

"If he had, he might still be alive, but he's dead as can be, with a bullet hole in his chest. Stratford and I found him when we went to order him to move out. There was nothing we could do about investigating it with the ship about to catch fire, so Stratford and Chin Ching moved the body there. You might wonder if you happened to see it. It's supposed to be under a sheet, but Robertshaw got nosy."

"Good God!"

"He found it and accused me of being a murderer, or at least an accomplice. He's a bit distraught. I think our situation has gotten to him. He's broken down, so I've ordered him to remain in his cabin. It's all cleared up now, and someday we'll have to have an investigation. Just one more little fuss, eh?"

"That's all you need, Captain, a murder investigation along with typhoons and earthquakes." He paused, patted his coat pocket, hesitated, and then continued in a subdued tone. "And another thing. Separation from someone special. I have a letter for you that she gave me just before she left. She asked me to hold it until she was well on her way." He pulled it out and handed it to Sam.

Sam took it in his hand and held it there for a moment, staring at it, then he looked up at Holden. "I—I—" he looked at the letter again.

"I'll leave you with it, Captain. That was my reason for coming. I'm sure she will be all right. She's a very brave woman."

"Yes she is," Sam said softly. "Thank you, Doctor, thank you."

Holden got up and left, and Sam sat for a long time looking down at the letter before opening it.

At last he ripped the envelope and began to read:

My dearest one,

This is goodbye. What else can I say? The only thing for me to do is go home to Sweden to get well, while you have so many responsibilities and duties (yes, that God damn duty!). And you have a beautiful new ship to command. You must be very proud of that. There is no other way now, but some day, maybe someday, we can be together again when life is simpler. I will never forget what we have had, and I will love you always.
Till someday—
Tak for love,
Mikaela

He read it through several times, then let it drop to the desk and lowered his head, bracing his forehead on his hand, with his elbow resting on the desk top. A terrible sadness filled him, a sense of loss and hopeless sorrow—yet she was right. Yes, she was right. Even without the implications in the letter to Robertshaw, there was no way they could have continued the relationship they had had for the past few months, the lovely moments of joy and sharing that had given a whole new focus to his life. Some women would have clung and demanded and made great scenes, yet Mikaela, with her infinite understanding, knew what could and could not be. If the earthquake hadn't torn their lives to pieces, they might have continued for a few more months, but it was a situation with no solution. And she had known.

He lifted his head and glanced around the sitting room, grunting at the sight of his collection of Oriental art and artifacts. How little they seemed to mean now, yet how they symbolized the life he had led, and, there was no question now, would continue to lead—granted, of course, that the *Monarch* was able finally to escape the perils of Yokohama Harbor. He shook himself, squared his shoulder consciously, and prepared to go out to the bridge. There was a long night ahead.

When Perkins relieved Barclay at 1800, he was still shaken from the reaction of the bosun in the motor launch. It was a nagging, sorrowing reminder of his action that morning, of the constant battle he had had in facing dangers, or even serious responsibilities. He couldn't free himself of the sense of shame and inadequacy. He had heard about the war, and about men fearing what their reaction would be in the first shock of combat, and he knew now the truth of it. Yet it wouldn't happen again, he swore to himself. He knew his weaknesses now, but he would be in control of them.

In his musings, he kept an occasional eye on the fires along the shore of the inner harbor. As evening twilight deepened and was replaced by darkness, areas that had just shown a plume of smoke in daylight now glowed, and flames could occasionally be seen leaping into the sky. Remembering what it had been like the night before, making his uneasy way through the ruins in darkness, he was glad that the ship was offshore. It would even be worse there tonight, he imagined.

After a while, he realized that the captain had come quietly out to the bridge wing and was standing at the rail in silence, peering off across the harbor at the fires on shore. Perkins didn't know what to say, but the captain finally broke the silence.

"Any developments, Mr. Perkins? The flames seem higher."

"I've been watching them, Captain. I'm not sure whether they are worse, or whether it's just the darkness that makes them look that way. They don't seem to be coming toward us."

Sam merely grunted in acknowledgement. After a silence, Perkins spoke again. "I'm sorry the kedging didn't work, Captain."

"It was a good try, but the bottom is too soft to hold the anchor."

"How can we get away from here, then?"

"We're hoping to have a dive team come in the morning to clear our port screw. That should free the rudder too, and we will be able to maneuver on our own. I just hope the propeller and rudder aren't seriously damaged."

"We can't get a tow to move our bow around?"

"I've been trying to locate tugboats all day, but none seems to be available. You saw what happened when that one did try to help us this morning. It takes a powerful vessel and good handling to move a ship of this size."

"Yes. I understand."

"I'm going below to confer with the doctors and Mr. Wheeler about the refugee situation. If we are to act as a relief station for the next few days, we will have to do a lot of special organizing. We can only feed 3,000 people for so long, and I'm sure we are low on medical supplies, even makeshift ones. There is a lot of work to be done."

"Yes sir, I'm sure."

"I will check here from time to time, but I want to be called immediately if there is any change in the situation. I shall be in the Yokohama Suite with Mr. Wheeler, but if you can't find me, Chin Ching will know where I am. He'll be standing by in my quarters."

"Aye, sir."

Sam told Chin Ching where he was going and went on down to the Yokohama Suite. He wanted to see what records Wheeler had made of the refugees.

Wheeler was busy at his desk, looking haggard and worried, and, like so many of the staff, needing a shave, but he was all business when Sam explained what he was after. While he was going over the lists Wheeler had compiled, Wheeler spoke to him.

"You'll be interested in one development, Captain. It concerns the Bridgeman children. I've been very worried about the poor tykes because the parents were good friends of mine. They seem to be completely orphaned—no relatives that I can find out about. But Miss Clare has asked to take temporary custody of them, and she has indicated that she would like to keep them permanently if it can be arranged."

"That's quite an order," Sam said in surprise. "That's very decent of the lady. I hope it can be worked out in some way if it seems to be for the best."

"Yes, so do I, and I do think it's a wonderful solution for the time being."

"Very good," Sam answered, and continued to go over the lists.

After a while, Wheeler spoke up again. "If you'll pardon my bringing it up, Captain Applebye, Mr. Stratford has told me of the situation with Mr. Davidoff, and with Mr. Robertshaw."

Sam stopped reading and turned to him slowly. "Yes?" he finally spoke.

"It is a very unfortunate situation, but I understand your action. I agree that it was the only way it could have been handled at the time."

"I'm glad you agree. It is a nasty business, and we will have to get at it, but with the ship in danger of going up in flames at any minute, there were other considerations that came first. I'm afraid the stress of our situation has affected Mr. Robertshaw's judgement, and I have ordered him to remain in his cabin. He seems quite distraught."

"So I understand. And I don't know what we would have done without you, Captain. I have marveled at the way you have taken the ship through some unbelievable crises."

"Thank you," Sam said gruffly. "Let's hope there are no more."

"Yes indeed," Wheeler added, and they went back to the lists.

Near the end of Perkins' watch he became aware that there was a much brighter glow over the inner harbor, with more flames visible. Evidently the fire on shore had spread to the oil on the water again, and, in the absence of any breeze, was eating its way slowly offshore. Perhaps, since the tide was ebbing, it was helping to move it, though where they were, the tide was not strong enough to swing the ship, and she still faced northwest. The captain had better see this, Perkins decided, and called for Chin Ching.

Sam was on the bridge in a matter of minutes, and Perkins pointed out the new situation. While they looked, the flames suddenly leaped higher, and a ball of fire swelled into the sky, with a great burst of sparks.

His eyes glued to the binoculars, Sam said, "It's got one of those abandoned lighters, or a coastal schooner."

The shower of sparks descended to the surface, and fiery bits of wreckage from the burning vessel soon started more fires in other pools of oil. A tongue of flames could be seen spreading across the area where the western jetty had subsided.

"By God, I knew this would happen," Sam muttered. "It has a way to go, but it's heading our way."

He studied it for a few more minutes, then turned to Perkins. "Mr. Perkins, get Mr. Barclay and tell him to organize the fire details. We have to be ready in case it does come this way. We still have oil around us here. God forbid," he finished, almost to himself.

Sam called the engine room to make sure they were on standby for getting underway. "I don't know where we can go except dead ahead until we run aground, but we have to be ready," he told Mr. Scott.

The ship soon erupted into a bustle of activity as the hose crews gathered their equipment on deck. The progress of the flames was extremely slow on such a night, and there was a good possibility that they would not come this far. It was better to wait for a while rather than to risk the panic that launching lifeboats would cause, but he did pass the order to Barclay to have the lifeboats outboard on davits and ready to go. This stir of activity would rouse the passengers and refugees, he knew, and they would have to be careful not to start a panic.

He kept constant watch on the fire while all the activity was going on, willing it to stay put, cursing inwardly at any sign of advance. With the binoculars to his eyes, he was aware of someone coming beside him but paid no attention until the man spoke.

"Captain?"

Sam turned impatiently and saw that it was Simms. "Yes, Simms?"

"We seem to be in a spot here, and I have an idea that might possibly help."

"What is that?"

"The yard tanker *Iris* from my old company is anchored off to starboard, abandoned, and I thought she might make a tugboat to bring your bow around and give you a clear shot at the outer bay."

"She's abandoned, you say. Who's to run her?"

"I can, if you lend me a couple of men. I used to operate her in my early days with the company. I know her well."

"Is she in operating condition?"

"I would think so. She was the morning of the quake, but I guess her crew panicked at all the fires and decided to get off her."

Sam looked at him silently for a long moment, then made up his mind. "It's worth a try if you're game."

"I'd rather try it than stay aboard here and be fried."

"I'll get you the bosun and a couple of seamen. They know how to handle the towing gear. Our motor lifeboat is still in the boom alongside. Mr. Perkins can take you over there." He paused. "You're sure, now?"

"Yes, sir."

"You see the situation? That we must get our bow about two points to starboard to give us a clear passage outside. Have you done any towing work yourself?"

"Some, in emergencies."

"You must get a long bit of line out by crossing our bow on an angle from port to starboard. I'd say at least sixty fathoms. I will have my anchor at short stay while you are getting ready, and we will weigh it just as you start your run. I will have slow ahead on my starboard screw after you take a strain so that we will not be a dead weight in inertia. Are you clear on this?"

"Yes, Captain, I am. From the look of the flames right now, I would say we should get right at it."

"Right you are. And you must be careful, I know, with the fuel oil aboard her."

Simms hesitated, then spoke. "It's not fuel oil. It's benzene."

Sam gave him a startled look. "Benzene. Good God." He paused looking at Simms in the eye. "Well. Do be careful."

"It's my neck," Simms muttered quietly.

"I hope she handles well. She's twin screw, isn't she?"

"No sir; single screw, but a powerful engine. She'll do the job."

Sam looked directly at him and shook his hand. "I thank you, and God be with you."

"You too, sir," Simms answered. "I'm off to the gangway. I'll meet your crew there."

"It'll be five minutes at most to collect them." He called Perkins and gave him his orders. "After you put Simms on the *Iris* you are to follow us out to the bay."

Simms left the bridge, went in the passageway to the captain's cabin, and spoke to Chin Ching. "I need something to write a letter."

Chin Ching gave him a pad and pen. Simms sat at the desk and wrote quickly. When he stopped, he turned to Chin Ching. "Will you watch me sign this, and put your name down that you did? Can you write your name in English?"

"Yes, sir."

"Good," Simms said, signing his name and handing the pen to Chin Ching. "Here, where I have written 'witness'. Now," he said, folding the letter into an envelope and giving it to Chin Ching, "I want you to hold this and give it to Captain Applebye in the morning."

"Yes, sir."

"Good man. Thank you. Be careful with it. Only to the captain. Now I'm off to save the ship." He stood up and left.

It was an anxious time on the bridge, as Sam watched the motor lifeboat pull away in the direction of the *Iris*. Just as it chugged away, there was a great flare-up in the area of the breakwater, and the flames, feeding on a new pool of oil, suddenly leaped out in their direction with increased speed, moving up on their starboard quarter. There was another fireball explosion as the flames caught up with an anchored vessel, and the cascade of burning debris spread the fire to new oil spills closer to them.

There was a wait that seemed endless until they saw lights go on aboard *Iris*. After another wait her anchor came up and her running lights could be seen. Sam ordered the cargo lights trained on the foredeck so that the crew working the towline could see clearly. The scene was as bright as day.

The way the flames were advancing, *Monarch*'s course out to the bay would be diagonally across them, and again, as in the morning, it was going to be a very near thing. Would *Iris* never get to them? She seemed to be taking forever, but finally she appeared, crossing *Monarch*'s stern and rounding up along the port side, with the ship's motor lifeboat trailing along. She came up under the port bow, her yellow funnel gleaming brightly in the *Monarch*'s lights, and the towline was passed down to her. There was a stout bollard at the stern of *Iris*, and Sam could see the seaman place the eye of the line over it. An extra puff of smoke from the yellow stack signalled that *Iris* was on her way at an angle off the starboard bow. Looking back at the firestorm on the water, Sam noticed that it was much closer, licking rapidly across new patches of oil and setting another anchored vessel on fire. He was beginning to feel the heat of it.

Monarch's anchor was weighed as soon as *Iris* took the line, and it was still under water, coming up, when *Iris* moved out off the bow. Sam ordered slow ahead on the starboard screw; it was just beginning to take hold as the towline came under strain. Holding his breath, he divided his attention between the towline and the advancing flames. The heat got stronger, and he felt the whirring whoosh as the fire fed on new oil and came ever closer.

This was the moment of truth. If *Iris* "hung up" and was drawn back against the *Monarch*, all was lost. There would be no time to start the process over before the flames caught them. He didn't think the ship's hoses would be a match for the fury of fire. Concentrating on the bow, he thought it would never indicate any change. The towline was taut, and great puffs of smoke were coming out of *Iris*' stack, but the ship's heading hadn't changed. Then, with a small, preliminary jerk, it moved just a bit to starboard. Gradually, the swing increased, though still painfully slow. Now the starboard screw was taking effect, and there was slight forward motion. One point! Halfway there! Just another ten or twelve degrees would do it. He checked the compass: NW x N now, and still swinging ever so slowly. Finally, there it was: NNW. She was in the clear and moving. He felt like giving a great cheer or blowing the whistle, but the firestorm was still too close off the starboard quarter, and he began to check its bearing against their forward motion.

Suddenly, there was a sharp crack, the towline flew high into the lights from the ship and swept across the foredeck like the lash of a whip. The crew fell flat, all just clear of its vicious sweep.

"It's parted," he groaned, and panic hit him for a moment until he realized that they were now on course and moving forward across the advance of the flames. *Monarch* was on her own.

"Look at *Iris*," the quartermaster yelled in alarm. "She's in trouble! Look at her!"

"The towline must have fouled her screw," Sam cried. "She looks out of control. She's coming back to us. We can't steer to miss her. It's too late."

There was no chance to reverse the screw or take any action, but Sam instinctively reached for the engine telegraph to stop the engine, knowing that it would not be in time.

Iris was right there under the starboard bow, and then she was crashing aft along the starboard side, heeling and spinning as the big ship went by her. Just as Sam watched in helpless horror, Robertshaw burst onto the bridge, his hair disheveled,his eyes wide. He pointed at the advancing flames and yelled, his voice a high shriek. "They'll get us! They'll get us! You're going to get us killed!"

Sam faced him squarely. "Mr. Robertshaw. Stop. That'll do. You are to stay in your cabin."

Robertshaw stared at him, his face contorted, his mouth working. "I won't be trapped there. I won't be trapped. You're trying to have me killed because I know about you and that woman."

He stumbled toward the rail and looked down at *Iris*, now just under the bridge as she careened and crashed along the hull. "That ship will be safer. She'll save me! Save me—" His voice broke in a high scream and he began to climb the rail. Sam made a desperate grab for him, but it was too late. Robertshaw cleared the rail, and his scream died out in the sound of the roaring wall of fire and the grinding thumps of *Iris* bashing toward the stern. She caromed off the *Monarch*'s quarter, rocking crazily, and the first lick of the advancing fire swept around her.

"Oh, God," Sam breathed.

The little ship disappeared into the flames, and, after a horrible moment of waiting, a huge fireball burst up from the inferno filling the sky, followed by the overwhelming whomp of an explosion that shook the *Monarch* from stern to stem and sent a blast of hot air sweeping across her decks. *Iris* disintegrated as pieces of wreckage flew high in the scarlet glare. When, glowing and giving off sparks, they fell back into the fire pool, the flames shot higher and continued to advance.

Sam slumped against the rail, drained and shaken. "Benzene," he murmured. "It was benzene. They saved us."

All he could do now was watch and pray, gauging the ship's forward speed against the angle of approach of the flames. Their roar intensified, and the heat was a force against his face. Hose details, working on the fantail, shot great sprays of water over the hull and decks, which hissed with steam as they hit.

Time seemed to stop as the deadly display crept up across the wake, but gradually he could tell that the ship was pulling away, and the flames were swallowing the wake, safely astern of the clouds of rising vapor.

In a few minutes the *Monarch* was steaming into clear, dark water, with a serene sky of stars above her and the Big Dipper over the bow. Almost in shock, functioning automatically, Sam gazed repeatedly astern at the diminishing flames marking the destruction of *Iris*. He conned the ship to an eight-fathom spot well out in the open waters of Tokyo Bay, where they dropped the anchor. The motor lifeboat had been following them and came alongside the boom as they anchored.

When all was secure, Sam stumbled to his cabin, still shaken into numb despair by the fate of *Iris*, his thoughts on Simms, the bosun, the two crewmen, and on Robertshaw's wild actions. He was barely able to respond when there was a knock on the door. The bosun walked in, hat in hand and a look of despair on his face.

"Good God, man," Sam cried. "I thought you were on *Iris*. What happened?"

The bosun bowed his head and answered in a low mumble.

"It was Mr. Perkins, sir."

"Perkins!"

"When we got to the *Iris* he ordered me to stay in the launch and said he was taking my place on *Iris*." He hesitated. "We—ah—he knew that I didn't think much of his guts, sir, after a couple of things that happened, and I guess he was showing me that I was wrong. I guess I was wrong."

Sam bowed his head. "The poor lad. He didn't have to do it."

"I'm sorry, sir."

"They're all gone, I guess. Simms, the two men—no way they could have lived through that blast."

"No sir. No way. It almost did for me in the boat. I was just far enough off." He paused. "I saw someone fall off the bridge. Who was that?"

"It was Robertshaw. He had lost his mind over the situation and he panicked."

"That's terrible." The bosun hung his head. "It was a near thing for us, sir."

"It was, it was. We owe all our lives to those men on *Iris*."

"I feel terrible about Mr. Perkins, sir."

"There's nothing you could have done. You're not to blame." He looked the bosun in the eye. "At least you're here. Thank God for that."

"Aye, sir." He turned slowly and went out.

While Sam was still trying to collect himself, Chin

Ching came in with a pot of tea. "I think you want this, sir," he said softly.

"Thank you. I probably could use a quart of scotch, too."

"I have this for you, Captain. Mr. Simms say give you in morning, but no have to wait now." He bowed his head, handed Sam the letter, and went out.

"What now?" Sam muttered as he unfolded it.

Captain Applebye:

I killed Davidoff. I am telling you this to save you trouble, because you have been a good friend, and maybe save someone innocent from investigation. If I survive this job, and I hope you are safe, I will go ashore in *Iris* and disappear through all the confusion to a new life somewhere else. My conscience is clear. I will never kill again, but the world is better off without Davidoff. He ruined many more lives than mine.

Martin Simms
Witness: Chin Ching

Sam stood tapping the letter against his hand for a long moment, then walked slowly out to the darkened wing of the bridge. Under the spread of stars above, the bay was calm, reflecting the light from above. The fires, now diminished, were a low glow back toward Yokohama. The ship was quiet, and he looked over the length of her, marveling at what she had been through. Off to the east was the open sea, where most of his life had been spent, and it was where Mikaela had gone when she left him. He stood looking out there for a long time, then turned slowly and went back to his cabin.

"God damn duty," he muttered. "God damn duty."

EPILOGUE

Oriental Monarch's port screw and rudder were cleared by a Japanese Navy diving team the following morning. She remained at Yokohama for a week as headquarters for refugees and relief administration. After re-fueling and re-supplying at Kobe, she left for Vancouver with her regular complement of passengers and received a hero's welcome on arrival.

Dr. Holden and Madelaine Clare married and adopted Peter and Susan. They settled in Newport Harbor, California, where he established a successful practice.

Mikaela went home to Sweden and lived with her parents until her son was of school age. She re-entered the foreign service and managed to get a position at the consulate in Seattle. After learning of Alicia Applebye's death, she wrote to Sam, who had retired as Senior C & O Captain from his last command, *Pacific Monarch*, at age 62. They were married and settled in a seaside cottage on Vancouver Island, near Victoria. Their son was a fighter pilot ace with the Royal Canadian Air Force in World War II, then became an airline pilot, and eventually the captain of jumbo jets.